Latter-day Spies
Rescue

Latter-day Spies
Rescue

a jungle adventure

Michele Ashman Bell

Covenant Communications, Inc.

Cover illustration by Brandon Dorman

Cover design copyrighted 2006 by Covenant Communications, Inc.

Published by Covenant Communications, Inc.
American Fork, Utah

Printed in Canada
First Printing: April 2006

12 11 10 09 08 07 06   10 9 8 7 6 5 4 3 2 1

ISBN 1-59811-093-4

DEDICATION

*This book is dedicated to
the lovely geese who help me
fly higher and farther
than I could on my own.
Thank you for being the wind
beneath my wings.*

ACKNOWLEDGMENTS

*I would like to express gratitude
to my husband, Gary, and my son, Weston,
for their help in the research of this book.
Thanks for making our trip to Brazil
a wonderful and unforgettable adventure.*

*I would also like to express gratitude to my
darling daughters, Kendyl, Andrea, and Rachel,
who keep me young and bring me joy.*

Chapter 1

THE RESCUE

"Where's Seth?" Sadie whispered through the darkness.

"I don't know," Fami answered. "He was just behind me."

"He probably stopped to eat something." Her brother's stomach was a bottomless pit.

Sadie slid her night-vision goggles onto her forehead and pushed a small button on her watchband that turned the face of her watch into a global positioning device. Inside the air vent shaft were two red flashing dots, representing herself and Fami. Twenty feet behind them was the third dot . . . Seth!

"I found him," she told Fami. "Back where the vent separated."

"Figures," Fami said. He was used to Seth always wanting to do things his own way. But now they needed to work as a team more than ever if they were to help save Mr. and Mrs. Fletcher from the terrorist group who had kidnapped them. There wasn't time to wait for reinforcements to arrive and help them. They were the Fletchers' only hope.

Using the same wristwatch, Sadie pushed another button activating the communication function. "T-2, this is T-1. What the heck are you doing? Over."

"I'm checking out this other option. Over."

"Negative, T-2. Bat and I have confirmed this is the correct location. Over."

Seth didn't answer.

Sadie waited a few more seconds to give him time to respond. The less time they were on their transmitters, the less chance they had of being discovered. Their code names, T-1 for twin number one, Sadie; and T-2 for twin number two, Seth; along with Bat, code name for Fami, kept them from being identified. The fact that Sadie was T-1 still irked Seth, but that was beside the point right now.

"T-2," Sadie said into her wristwatch, "immediate response requested. Over."

"I'm right behind you." Seth's voice startled Sadie.

She turned and looked at her brother in the dim glow from their transmitters. "We don't have time for this."

"I wanted to make sure we were taking the right tunnel," he said. "I don't think this is the way to Mom and Dad."

"Listen!" Fami hissed.

The three kids froze, straining to hear the noise. A faint whirring and clicking echoed through the vent.

"This way," Sadie said. Then she turned to her brother. "Stay with us!"

"I will!" Seth snarled.

A faint light began to fill the air shaft.

Fami turned and put his fingers to his lips. They were getting close to the source of the noise.

After creeping slowly along the shaft, they neared an opening that was covered by a metal grate. Fami moved aside, allowing Sadie the first glimpse.

"A computer room," she said. "I can't tell if anyone's inside."

Seth peered through the slats of the grate. "It's the control room. There are monitors showing the grounds outside and different areas inside the building."

"That means there are guards somewhere," Fami said.

"That also means we can find out where they're keeping Mom and Dad," Sadie replied. She thought for a moment. "Seth, you need to crawl to the next opening and see what kind of trouble you can stir up. Hopefully that will pull the guards from their station so I can check the monitors."

Seth hesitated.

"Now!"

"Okay," he said as he began to inch silently away. Fami stayed behind with Sadie.

A voice inside the room below drifted through grate. "Hey, Jantzen, wake up. You're supposed to be on guard."

Sadie and Fami barely breathed as they listened.

"Here's your sandwich," the man continued. "Anything on the monitors?"

"Nah, nothin'." The guard named Jantzen stretched his arms overhead. They hadn't seen him because he'd been slumped down low in his chair. "It's as quiet as a church today." There was a crinkling of wrappers and the click and fizz of a can of soda pop being opened. "Hey, I told you I wanted ham and Swiss on whole wheat."

"Sorry," the other man replied. "They only had turkey and cheddar, or tuna fish. If you don't like it, next time get your own sandwich."

"Did you at least remember to get mustard?" Jantzen asked. "I gotta have mustard."

"Tell you what, I'll cover your post while you go get what you need so you can quit your whining."

"Hey, I can't help it if I'm particular about my sandwiches," Janzten said, scooting his chair back with a loud screech.

"Pick me up some chips while you're there, will ya?"

Janzten grunted a reply and left the room. The guard bit into his sandwich, leaned back in his chair, and propped his feet lazily on the counter. He chomped down a few bites of his sandwich when, suddenly, an alarm sounded. One of the monitors flashed a red warning signal.

Sadie and Fami nudged each other. Seth had done his job.

The guard made an announcement over a loudspeaker and raced from the room.

Knowing they only had a split second to check the monitors and computer system to find her parents, Sadie steeled herself for entry into the room.

Fami helped her remove the grate from the vent and, with the use of a nylon rope they had with them, lowered her through the ceiling into the room.

Once Sadie's feet touched the ground, she went straight to the computer and began navigating the system for any sign of her parents' location in the building.

"Any luck?" Fami asked.

"No," she replied, her fingers shaking. The men would be back any minute. "I can't find anything in the computer."

"What about the monitors? Did you check them?"

"Fami, I know what I'm doing," she snapped. Panic sent her heart racing and made her palms sweat. She glanced up at the monitors as she pulled in a calming breath, and, suddenly, right in front of her face were the images of her parents, tied into chairs that were back-to-back.

Chiding herself for not listening to Fami, she announced, "I found them," then quickly accessed the layout of the building to find the location where her parents were being held.

Before she cleared the screen, she changed the setting on the monitor to replay the last thirty minutes of recorded footage. She just hoped it was long enough.

With the push of a button, she cleared the computer screen and jumped up from her chair.

"Let's go get them," she said, grabbing hold of the rope.

Using the knots that were spaced twelve inches apart, she climbed the rope back up through the ceiling as Fami held it firmly.

She quickly rejoined him in the shaft, and they pulled up the rope as the sound of men's voices came their direction.

"The grate!" Sadie whispered. She and Fami picked up the heavy grate and slid it into place just as the men burst into the room.

"I say it was just a malfunction. That power surge we had earlier probably messed up the timers on the alarm system," Jantzen explained.

"I don't know. Something tells me something fishy's going on. We'd better keep a sharp eye out. The last guys who didn't detect an intruder still haven't been released from the hospital."

"Do a quick security check on the computer while I check the monitors," Jantzen instructed.

"Let's go," Sadie whispered so only Fami could hear.

Without making a sound, they crawled along the shaft until they were a distance from the security room. Sadie stopped long enough to make contact with her brother.

"I know where they are," she told him over the transmitter.

"I'll be right there," he answered.

Seth joined them in the shaft, and Sadie quickly explained to her brother what she'd seen on the screen. He had an uncanny knack for understanding building layouts and position.

"We need to follow this shaft," he began.

"Listen!" Fami interrupted. Voices drifted through the shaft. They were faint, but something about them sounded familiar.

"It's your dad," Fami said. "I'm sure of it."

"Then let's go," Seth said. He started in the direction of the voices, but Sadie stopped him.

"Something doesn't feel right," she cautioned.

"Sadie, it's them. We have to rescue them."

"I know."

"Then what's the problem? Let's go."

"Fami," Sadie said, "what do you think?"

"There is danger if we go ahead and danger if we stay. I think we need to keep our eye on our goal."

His words made sense. Danger was all around them, and who knew what would happen to their parents the longer they remained locked in that room?

"Okay," she surrendered. "Let's go."

Staying close together, they crawled toward the sound of the voices, which grew louder and clearer the nearer they got.

Sadie's heart pounded wildly in her chest. She couldn't explain it, but something didn't feel right.

Just then, Seth let out a startled scream and disappeared down the heat vent.

"Seth," Fami called, making the mistake of crawling forward one more step. He slid downward as the vent made a sudden drop. "Help!" he cried. Turning, he grabbed at Sadie to stop himself from sliding, but he only succeeded in taking her with him.

She stifled a scream as they made the terrifying ride through darkness, the vent groaning and creaking under their weight. The ride came to an abrupt halt, and they landed in a heap on the ground inside some kind of cavern. It smelled musty of moisture and mold.

"Get off," Seth growled, giving Fami and Sadie a strong push with his hands and feet.

Dim lights on the walls gave an eerie glow to the cavern.

Seth stood, grateful that no bones had been broken, and looked straight at a metal door that was bolted shut. He took a step toward the door.

"Stop!" Sadie cried.

Seth froze, then looked down at a low laser beam that ran across the front of the door about one foot from the ground.

"Whoa, that was close. Good thing you have those glasses."

"Yeah, except we have another problem," Fami told him.

"What?" Seth asked.

"The doorknob," Sadie said.

"What about it?" Seth questioned.

Sadie studied the doorknob closely. More than anything, she didn't want it to be what she thought it was, but the glowing red numbers on the time bomb strapped to the door read four minutes and fifty-eight seconds.

Chapter 2
The Test

"Are you kidding me?" Seth exclaimed. "A bomb?" He checked the time on the explosive. "We're never going to make it."

"Seth, stop talking. That's not helping at all," Sadie scolded. "We need to see if Mom and Dad are in there."

"Just don't touch the door," Fami said. "The bomb might be sensitive to vibration."

Sadie nodded. Then, standing as near to the door as she dared, she said, "Mom? Dad? Are you in there?" Then she quickly added, "If you are, don't touch the door. Just answer."

The three kids listened but heard nothing.

"Mom? Dad?" she said again.

"Sadie?" a voice replied on the other side of the door.

"Mom!"

"Honey, it's too dangerous. You kids save yourselves. You need to get out of here."

"We're not leaving, Mom," Seth answered. "We're getting you out of there. Hey," he exclaimed as he felt water trickling around his feet, "the floor is covered with water."

"I think we need to get out of here as soon as possible," Fami said.

"Mom and Dad," Sadie called, "try and get as far away from the door as you can. And find cover."

"Do you think you can diffuse the bomb?" Seth asked his sister.

Sadie studied the device one more time as the seconds ticked away. "Fami, do you still have that pen with the magnetic strip on it?" Sadie asked.

Fami dug into his pocket and found the pen, then handed it to her.

"I hear more water coming in," Seth said. "We'd better hurry."

Sadie shushed him. "I'm trying to concentrate."

Holding her breath, Sadie carefully placed the special magnetic strip across the front of the numbers, and, just as she'd hoped, the numbers froze into position. The ticking stopped.

"Yes!" Fami said when the device went quiet.

Breathing a sigh of relief, Sadie said a quick prayer of thanks and asked for additional heavenly help. She was going to need it.

"The ground is covered in water," Seth said.

"Seth, please," Sadie said, trying to concentrate on her next move to diffuse the bomb.

"I think it's rising," Seth said.

Sadie looked at the ground. Her brother was right.

"I have a question," Fami said. "What happens when the water gets as high as the laser beam?"

Seth and Sadie looked at each other with matched expressions of fear.

"Get that bomb diffused!" Seth exclaimed to his sister.

Seth kept watch on the beam as Sadie carefully leaned over it and took the round explosive device in her hand. It was the size of a nightstand alarm clock, but not very heavy.

The wiring looked familiar and simple enough. Each wire served a purpose; she just had to figure out which ones to cut. From her belt, she unclipped a piece of high-tech equipment that resembled a Swiss army knife with myriad extra functions.

She pressed a button, and a small pair of needle-nosed wire clippers extended. Sadie began to eliminate the color-coded wires one by one: black, red, white, and green. That left the yellow and the blue. One of them would sever the circuit, allowing the bomb to stop working; the other would cause the bomb to detonate.

"The water's getting close to the level of the laser," Seth said.

"I'm working as fast as I can." Her nerves sent her heartbeat racing.

"Sadie," Fami said in a calm voice. "Is there anything we can do to help?"

"I've narrowed it down to the yellow and blue wires. I just have to figure out which one stops the explosion and which one kills us all instantly."

"You'd better think fast," Seth said. "Mom? Dad?" he yelled. "Are you okay?"

"Get us out of here," their father hollered back.

"Sadie!" Seth urged.

"I know, I know," Sadie cried. "I don't know which one to cut."

"You can do it. Follow your instincts," Fami said with reassurance.

"I think it's the blue. I'm ninety-nine percent sure it's the blue."

"Then cut it," Fami said.

Sadie shut her eyes and swallowed. She didn't dare. She wasn't one hundred percent sure.

"Hurry, Sadie," Seth said. "The water's almost there."

"Cut it," Fami encouraged. "I have faith in you."

Sadie couldn't bring herself to cut the wire. She didn't trust her instincts. What if she was wrong?

"Cut it," Seth yelled. "Before it's too—"

Waaa, waaa, waaa, waaa. The shrieking alarm was so loud they had to cover their ears. Red lights flashed all around them. The door in front of them slid open, and she saw the disappointed look on the faces in front of her.

It was over. She'd failed the test. If this whole thing had been real, they would have been captured or killed. Either way, it was a bad situation.

Sadie couldn't look up at Mr. Beauregard, the spy-training instructor.

"You three meet me in my office as soon as you change into dry clothes."

* * *

The spy school where Seth, Sadie, and Fami were receiving special training was located in a secret location somewhere outside of London. They took every bit of their training seriously. They'd been left to their own devices for survival enough times that their parents all agreed that the children needed to be able to protect themselves and know what to do if they ever found themselves in difficult or life-threatening situations again.

Along with their month-long training in basic self-defense and survival skills, they had been trained in the use of high-tech gadgets. Fami had received a pair of glasses, designed specifically for him, to aid with his vision impairment. Highly skilled specialists had performed dozens of tests on Fami to discover the extent of the damage to his sight caused by the lightning. The results had been startling. The doctors were convinced that one day his vision would return. His body just needed time to heal and compensate for the damage. Until then, the glasses they gave him intensified his ability to distinguish between contrasts of light and dark. He was now able to see outlines and images of people and objects. His world was still in black and white, but he didn't care—he felt as though he'd been given miracle glasses. He finally could get around without much trouble. He still couldn't read small print or play video games, but Fami felt a huge amount of freedom not having to depend upon others just to get across the room and sit in a chair or find his shoes in the morning.

"Listen," Fami said as the three of them walked down a long corridor to Beauregard's office. "It's no big deal. We'll pass the virtual test next time."

"There won't be a next time. Our training's over. It's all my fault," Sadie said for the thousandth time. "I'm a horrible mission leader. Why was I put in charge?"

"Sadie, will you stop it?" Seth countered. "As hard as it is for me to say this, you took us farther than we even thought we'd get on that mission. You have better skills in diffusing bombs than either of us. But we're a team. Fami and I are just as responsible as you are. We've been trained the same as you have."

"But I choked. When everything was on the line, I choked."

"We probably won't ever have to figure out which wire to cut to diffuse a bomb anyway," Fami said. "I mean, our parents barely let us go to the bathroom alone. I doubt we'll ever be any-where without protection and armed guards around us. Besides, you know the rule, we're always supposed—"

"—to call the authorities first, I know. But if help can't get to us in time, we're on our own. And I wanted to pass the virtual test this time before we left the program. I wanted to clear all the levels of training," Sadie said.

"That was the highest level, Sadie, and the only reason they even let us try was because you begged them. Hardly anyone passes the expert level before they leave. We will still graduate from the course with some of the highest marks the school has given out. We should be proud of our-selves," Seth insisted, obviously not wanting to add to his sister's frustration. "We're spy school graduates. That's so amazing! I'm going to be a superspy when I grow up."

Sadie groaned at her brother's enthusiasm. "Don't you understand?" Sadie insisted. "We seem to get caught in bad situations whether we want to be or not. It's possible we will use this stuff sometime in our lives. I don't want anyone dead because of me!"

"Lighten up, already. We have nothing to be ashamed of. But if you don't want to be team leader, I guess I can do it."

"That's fine with me," Sadie said. "Be my guest. I don't want the responsibility."

"What about Cleopatra?" Fami said. Even Fami's rat had received training in the program. She was as intelligent and capable as any of the other animals in the program, most being trained for police work to sniff out drugs and explosives. Cleopatra had proven herself useful in the past more than once, and all three of the kids knew she was a valuable member of their team.

"She's probably smarter than all of us combined," Seth joked as he dug into his pocket and pulled out a Snickers bar. He'd brought half a suitcase full of treats with him for the intense training program, and he was down to his last bag of candy. As far as Seth was concerned, when the candy was gone, it was time to go home.

"It's true," Fami said to Sadie. "Our parents aren't having us do this program because they plan to send us on secret missions and stuff. It's just in case we ever get in a bind like we have in the past. Then we'll know better what to do. But they keep such a close watch on us now, we probably won't ever need to use these skills."

"I guess you're right," she finally agreed. "But for a moment, even though it was just pretend, I held the lives of five people in my hands. It was a horrible feeling to know that I was responsible for everyone's future."

"You're putting way too much pressure on yourself, Sadie." They stopped in front of Beauregard's office door. "We're here," Seth said. "We'll just face him together, and it will be okay."

"You go first," Fami said, giving Seth a little push from the back.

"Why me?" Seth resisted.

"Because he likes you the best."

Seth smiled. "You think so?" He tapped on the door.

"Come in," answered a voice from inside the room.

The kids each took a turn putting their hand on the green-screen palm reader, which confirmed their identity before they entered the room.

They filed inside and stood, shoulder to shoulder, facing Mr. Beauregard's large desk. The man's black leather chair was turned away from them, but they knew he was there because he was talking on the phone.

Less than a minute later, he said good-bye and turned forward to greet the three students.

"Please, sit down," he said.

Mr. Beauregard stood, his six-foot-five frame towering over them. His black wool suit strained against his broad shoulders. The fluorescent lighting from the ceiling reflected off his bald head. With no expression on his face, he addressed them. "You failed your mission. What have you got to say for yourselves?"

Sadie looked down at her hands in her lap. Fami squirmed in his chair. Seth cleared his throat and grasped the arms of the chair as if ready to bolt from the room.

"Well?"

"It was my fault, sir." Sadie lifted her chin courageously and looked directly into his eyes. She knew it was her fault, and she knew Mr. Beauregard knew it. There was no point in trying to get out of it.

"I thought you were a team."

"We are, sir."

"Then no individual takes the blame. If a team works as it's supposed to, the team takes full responsibility for success as well as for failure."

"Yes, sir," Sadie said, looking back down.

"Your time here with us ends tomorrow," he said. "Fami."

Fami's head snapped up. "Uh, yes, sir."

"You've proven to have strengths with languages and communication devices. You are also quite good with hand-to-hand combat. You must work on all of your skills. A team would benefit greatly from your strengths. Continue to hone your skills."

"I will, sir. Thank you."

"Seth."

"Sir." Seth looked at the man addressing him.

"I understand you have the highest score in maneuvers that require aim and accuracy. You show a natural instinct for directions, maps, and locations."

"Yeah, it's kind of weird—"

"This, too, is valuable for a team," Mr. Beauregard interrupted. "Keep your skills sharp with practice and continued studying. Knowledge is power. The more you know, the stronger you become."

"Yes, sir."

"Sadie."

Sadie remained looking at her hands in her lap.

"The pressure got to you today."

Sadie nodded.

"Keep practicing, Sadie. If you learn to stay calm under pressure, I promise you will make a great team leader."

"What?" Seth exclaimed.

"I don't understand, sir," she said. "Our mission failed."

"You have shown exceptional skills with computers and technical devices," he continued as though he had not been interrupted.

She looked back down at her hands. Earlier that day, her skills hadn't been so exceptional.

"Even with bombs."

She shrugged, hoping someday to be able to put the whole experience behind her.

"Life is full of surprises. Do you remember what we taught you the first day you arrived at the training center?"

"Always expect the unexpected," Sadie said.

"That's right. That way you'll always be prepared for whatever happens. You children have shown that you have fortitude, ingenuity, and courage. With the skills you've learned here, you will be better prepared to face anything life hands you. Due to the nature of your fathers' positions, I can guarantee that you will find occasion to call upon these skills in the future. Practice and review each day."

"We will, sir," Seth replied.

"That will be all. You'll need to have your gear packed by 0800 in the morning."

Mr. Beauregard approached Fami and shook his hand. "How is the Image Contrast Intensifier working?"

"Works great, sir."

"I hope your sight returns someday, but if not, I want you to know I've never met anyone with a physical challenge who has risen above it like you have."

Fami nodded and smiled broadly.

Mr. Beauregard then shook Seth's hand.

"I understand that our cook is convinced your legs are hollow. Did you really eat an entire pan of lasagna yourself?"

"Not all in one sitting, sir."

Mr. Beauregard chuckled. "Don't let your appetite rule your judgment, young man."

"I won't, sir."

He then stood in front of Sadie.

"Not many of our students have passed the expert-level mission on the first try," he told her.

"But I wanted to, sir."

He shook her hand. "You remind me of myself at your age."

Sadie raised an eyebrow with confusion.

"Never being satisfied with anything but your best is a wonderful quality in a person. It can also make life very frustrating at times."

"I'm learning that very quickly, sir," she replied.

Mr. Beauregard smiled and nodded in under-standing. "Tell your parents hello for me," he told the children, who turned and began walking toward the door. "Oh, Sadie, could you stay just a moment?"

Seth and Fami looked at her.

After they left, Mr. Beauregard addressed her again. "I have a concern I'd like to talk to you about."

Chapter 3

SURPRISE

Mr. Beauregard's voice was kind and caring, almost fatherly. "Sadie, I'm concerned that you are being too hard on yourself about what happened today, and I don't want you to leave our program feeling like you're a failure."

Sadie's mouth dropped open. "But it was my fault—"

"There's no *I* in the word *team*," he said. "As you three work together, you'll learn how to balance out one another, help each other, build each other's strengths. And as for you, well," he paused, "you are just beginning to understand how important it is to trust your instincts. Your confidence in yourself and your judgment will grow as you exercise your judgment and make correct choices. You're bound to make a few wrong choices along the way."

"Like today."

"Maybe."

"Maybe?" Sadie didn't understand.

"You didn't actually choose today, did you?"

"You mean which color of wire to cut? How did you—"

"We watched the entire time on hidden cameras."

"Oh." She looked down at her shoes.

"What color of wire were you going to cut, Sadie?"

She didn't answer.

"Sadie?"

"Blue," she said softly.

When he didn't answer right away, she looked up, expecting to see disappointment in his eyes. Instead, she saw kindness.

"Your instincts were right."

Her eyes opened wide. "Blue was the right one?"

He nodded.

Even though she hadn't followed through with cutting the wire, diffusing the bomb, and saving the day, she felt like celebrating. She had chosen the right color. And she took comfort in knowing that her instincts had been right.

"Focus each day on listening to that inner voice. The more you pay attention and follow the promptings you receive, the better you will become at recognizing them."

Sadie knew that the main reason her parents allowed them to come to this particular training center was that Beauregard was not only a family friend, but also a member of their faith.

"I was proud of you three today. You are a few years younger than most of our recruits, and you've had a rigorous training schedule," Mr. Beauregard told her. "There is nothing to be ashamed of by your performance."

"Thank you, sir." Sadie lifted her head high as she shook the man's hand.

"You've been given many wonderful gifts, young lady. And where much is given, much is required. Do you understand that?"

"Yes."

"Good. Now, you'd better get going so you can catch up with the others." He looked at her with a smile. "You kids stay in touch, okay? And keep an eye on that brother of yours. He's got some great skills, but his confidence exceeds his abilities."

"Yes, sir, I will. And thank you, Mr. Beauregard."

* * *

The ride to the airport was quiet. Each of the kids was filled with conflicting emotions. As difficult and stressful as the training program had been, they'd had more fun in those four weeks than they had ever known. It had been exciting and educational, terrifying but also interesting. They'd gone rappelling off sixty-foot towers, learned hand-to-hand combat techniques, and been trained in the use of audio and video surveillance techniques. Their training in unarmed defense tactics and silent movement techniques had been intense and merciless, but they knew that each skill they learned better prepared them for the unexpected, which seemed to happen to them more often than not.

Aside from their global positioning/communicator watches, they'd also received a private supply of gadgets to help them develop their skills and equip them with lifesaving abilities. Fami's ICI glasses even had a special feature that allowed him to see what was behind him. Seth and Sadie also had sunglasses that allowed them to see behind them. They had regular binoculars and a small earpiece to receive sounds out of range of their normal hearing. They had a small pistol that shot out steel cording to create a zip line, complete with a set of handles. Learning to use the zip pistol had been one training session they could have done over and over, it had been so much fun. Sadie also loved the spy-cam pen that could easily be hooked up to a computer to see the images. It also wrote in the dark and used invisible ink.

But just as Mr. Beauregard had said, they needed to practice their skills daily. Just because they
had fancy gadgets didn't mean they didn't need to
know how to work all the items and that they
wouldn't forget some of the important training
they'd received in other aspects of their training.
They'd learned basic functions for all of the
equipment, but there were more complicated
functions they needed to learn. And since their
formal training was completed, they would have
to learn these functions by reading the manuals
and practicing the skills outlined in the manuals.

"Where are your parents meeting us?" Seth
asked, clicking his watch to show a grid layout of the
route they were driving from the training center to
the airport.

"At the United counter," Fami replied, unable
to take his eyes off the passing view of the city. He
had told his parents a little bit about his glasses,
but they had no idea what a great help they'd
been to his ability to see. Ever since his father had
returned to their family, he hadn't stopped
dreaming about finding a way to restore Fami's
sight. Now that the experts at the training school
had run tests to determine the extent of damage
to Fami's eyes—and concluded that, indeed, one
day his vision would be restored again—that
dream might actually come true. Fami couldn't
wait to tell his parents when he saw them.

"I'm going to miss that place," Seth said. "The food was great there."

"What about all the stuff we learned? I still haven't read the manual that explains all the functions for our equipment. Like our watches and the earpieces. We really should understand completely what their capabilities are," Sadie told him.

"I know," Seth said. "Why don't you read the manuals and teach us."

"How are you ever going to be a superspy if you won't even read a simple instruction manual?" Sadie asked her brother with irritation.

"Gut instinct," he replied. "I have the mind of a superspy."

Sadie rolled her eyes.

"I couldn't believe how serious some of those older kids were about becoming spies," Fami said. "It's weird to think that someday Paul Galetti could actually be a foreign spy in the Middle East or Russia. Or that little Millie Lucas could help break spy codes or go undercover to destroy drug rings in Columbia or illegal activity somewhere in Asia or something."

"I'm not going to be a spy," Sadie said. "I'm going to become a designer and design shoes and purses that all the celebrities want to wear to the Academy Awards and stuff."

"No one in the entire world is going to pay you to do that, Sadie," Seth said.

"You wait, Seth. I'll be a famous designer someday." What did her brother know about fashion? He couldn't even match his socks with his shirt.

"What about you, Fami?" Seth asked. "What do you want to be when you grow up?"

"If I could be anything, I'd be an astronaut," he said. "By the time I'm an adult, who knows what kind of space travel we'll be capable of? I could be the first man on Mars or help build a space station on the moon or something."

"Wow, Fami," Seth said. "That would be awesome, but wouldn't it be hard if you can't . . . you know, you can't . . ."

"See?" Fami shook his head. "No, I can't be an astronaut if I can't see, but there are still a lot of things I can do when I grow up." He paused. "Until then I am going to learn everything I can about science and space travel, just in case my full sight returns."

Seth and Sadie exchanged looks. Fami rarely ever talked about his sight being a handicap or hindrance to his ability to do the things he wanted. But by the sound of his voice, they both knew he was disappointed at the thought that his dream of being an astronaut might not come true.

Their car followed the exit to the airport and wound through the congested lanes of traffic.

"It's going to be weird to go back to our home and see all the damage from the fire," Sadie said.

"Yeah, I'll bet all our stuff smells like smoke," Seth said, then turned and looked out the window. They were nearing the terminal entrance. He was excited to see Fami's parents again. Fami's father, Robert Laningham, had gone into hiding through the Witness Protection Program in an effort to protect his family. The men he'd been responsible for putting behind bars had threatened his life and the lives of his family. By allowing them to think he was dead, he'd hoped they would leave his wife and son alone. But that hadn't been the case. Mr. Laningham had ultimately decided he could do more to protect his family by being with them than by remaining in hiding and allowing them to fend for themselves. There was no one more surprised than Fami when he arrived in Hawaii with the Fletcher family, thinking he was meeting his mother, but finding his father there also.

They'd all spent a relaxing week in Hawaii enjoying the water and the sun. But as soon as they'd left, they were taken to London to attend the Spy Training Academy. Both sets of parents wanted their children equipped with the skills and tools needed to keep themselves safe. Whether they liked it or not, they were targets of an organized crime and terrorism group that seemed to have members in every corner of the world, no matter how remote. It was a group capable of anything.

The van pulled up to the curb in front of the entrance, and the kids piled out. Their driver, employed by the Spy Training Academy, helped them unload their bags, then escorted them to meet Fami's parents.

Pulling their suitcases behind them, the three kids followed the driver into the airport and looked for the United counter. The terminal was huge and crowded with swarms of people.

"I believe the counter is this way," the driver said.

Walking side by side, with Fami between Seth and Sadie, the three followed the driver toward the United counter.

"Fami!" a voice called. The kids looked to see Mr. and Mrs. Laningham hurrying in their direction. The driver stepped out of the way as the kids and Fami's parents greeted each other.

"We're so glad you made it safely," Mr. Laningham said, pulling his son into a giant hug.

Mrs. Laningham hugged each of the Fletcher kids, then the two parents switched.

"Look, Mom," Fami said. "These are the Image Contrast Intensifiers I told you about. Top secret," he whispered. "I'll tell you more when we can talk in private."

Mr. Laningham reached into his pocket for some money to tip the driver, but the man had disappeared without them even knowing it.

"Well, so much for that," Mr. Laningham said. "I forget how careful even the employees have to be about being recognized. He's certainly good, isn't he?"

The kids nodded. The entire staff at the academy was highly trained in their specific skills, many of them retired military personnel or secret agents.

"We can't wait to hear all about your training," Mr. Laningham said. "But first we need to get checked in. Our plane leaves soon."

"I can't wait to get home," Sadie said. "I feel like we've been gone forever. After we get checked in, can I call my mom and dad?"

Peredot and Robert Laningham looked at each other and then at Sadie, both of them remaining silent.

"What?" Sadie said, feeling her stomach muscles tighten.

"Well, kids, your parents have decided you aren't going back to Germany just yet," Mr. Laningham said.

"Huh?" Seth said.

"Why not?" Sadie questioned.

"They didn't tell you how much of your house was destroyed in the fire because they didn't want you to worry while you were at the training academy."

"How much was destroyed?" Sadie asked.

The Laninghams looked at each other again, then Mrs. Laningham spoke. "It could take several months to make the repairs. Most of your belongings were damaged by smoke and water."

"I'm sorry, kids," Mr. Laningham said, putting his arm around Seth's shoulders. Mrs. Laningham gave Sadie a hug. "It's going to be okay, though. Your parents are taking care of everything."

"Did they catch the guys who did it, Dad?" Fami asked.

"They have some leads," Mr. Laningham replied. "We're positive it wasn't an accident and that the men were sent by—"

"Bachmann?" Seth asked as anger swelled inside of him.

"I'm afraid so," Mr. Laningham said.

"What is it going to take to get those guys to leave us alone?" Sadie asked.

"We're trying to find the answer to that as quickly as we can," Mr. Laningham told her.

"So, if we can't go home, then where are we going?" Sadie asked, fighting back the emotion that felt like a knot in her throat.

"Do you remember our good friend Luciano Jaderson, from Brazil?"

"The one who dresses in those funny gaúcho clothes?" Seth answered.

"Yes, that's the one," Mr. Laningham said. "He's invited us for a visit. Your parents are joining us in São Paulo, then we will travel to his home in southern Brazil together. We also have some business to attend to while we are there."

"Wait a minute. Did you say southern Brazil?" Sadie said.

Mrs. Laningham closed her eyes for a moment as if searching for the right words. After a short pause, she looked at them and said, "Children, this is so much for you to digest all at once. I am sorry we have to burden you with all of this. Your parents don't feel it's safe for you to return home right now. Luciano lives in a very remote, safe place. He has many guards around his house. Your parents have discussed this with us at great length, and we feel this is the best solution."

"Wow," Seth said, releasing a big breath. "How much more bizarre can our lives get?"

"Don't ask," said Sadie. "Our luck might get even worse."

"Worse?" Seth exclaimed. "How could it possibly get worse?"

"Since we're going to be spending so much time together in the future, we can dispense with the formalities," Mr. Laningham told them. "You can call me Rob," he said.

"You can call me Peredot," Fami's mother followed up.

"Hey, Dad," Fami burst in. "You said you had some business there too. What kind of business?"

"That is something we can talk about on the plane, son. Let's get checked in." Rob looked at the children, whose expressions reflected their confusion. "I promise, we will answer all of your questions when we can talk more privately."

Chapter 4

BUMPY RIDE

Sadie tried to concentrate on her magazine, but her mind kept wandering. It didn't help that there was a ton of turbulence.

"You know, we're over the ocean," Seth told her. "If the plane goes down, we die."

"Thank you for sharing, Seth. Now, will you please not talk to me the rest of the way?" They still had eight hours of flight time ahead of them. Sadie scooted as far away from him as her seat belt would allow. She didn't want him to think the turbulence was making her nervous, but in all honesty, it was. Having him point out the potential of them dying at sea didn't help.

She looked up and saw Fami making his way toward them. He'd gone to visit with his parents and was getting back to his seat just in time—they were about to serve dinner.

Jumping up, Sadie offered her seat to Fami so he could sit next to her brother. It was a mean thing to do to Fami, but he tolerated Seth much better than she did.

Fami expelled a loud breath as he slid into their row. "That was weird. In fact, this whole trip is weird." Fami sat down and buckled his seat belt.

"What's weird?" Seth asked, wondering if the little kid sitting behind him was going to kick his seat the entire flight to São Paulo.

"Do you remember my dad saying they had some business in Brazil to take care of while we are there?"

"Yeah," Seth answered, wondering if the kid would stop kicking his seat if he reclined it really fast.

"I guess this Luciano guy is a soybean farmer, and my dad wants to check out his farm."

"Why?" Seth asked.

"He might be interested in starting up his own business."

"In soybeans? You mean like your dad would become a farmer and you guys would move there?" Seth didn't like where this conversation was going.

Fami nodded. "Yeah. Dad thinks it's a good idea. He's always loved Brazil, since he served his mission there, and both of my parents speak Portuguese."

"But you can't move to Brazil," Seth said. "We're a team. What are they—" Then he gasped.

"What?" Sadie said, alarmed.

"What if Mom and Dad want to move there too?"

"They aren't going to make us move to Brazil. We can't even speak the language."

"That didn't matter when we moved to Germany," Seth countered.

Sadie got a heavy feeling in the pit of her stomach. Seth's reasoning made sense.

"If we have to move, it would be best if we could move together," Fami said.

"Who wants to move to a soybean farm?" Seth exclaimed. "I don't even know what soybeans are used for, except that disgusting tofu junk in Chinese food. And if we lived clear down there, how would I ever work on my spy skills? I've got to keep them honed and sharp," he said, sliding on his rear vision sunglasses and sitting up tall so he could look over his seat.

"You know what?" Sadie said. "Just like we learned in training, we have to stay calm. We'll just wait and see what's going on before we over-react, okay?"

"Okay," Seth answered unenthusiastically. Then he suddenly erupted with joy. "They're bringing food." The flight attendants finally delivered their meal, and the conversation was dropped for the time being. But it weighed heavy on each of their minds. What was this trip all about?

* * *

"Stop!" Seth exclaimed, waking Sadie up from a dead sleep.

"What's going on?" she fumed. "I was asleep!"

"I can't take it anymore!" Seth told her. Turning around in his seat, he looked over the top at the little boy sitting behind him. "Could you please stop kicking the back of my chair?" Seth said.

The little boy looked up at Seth, then his bottom lip began to tremble, and he suddenly burst into tears. Seth's expression grew alarmed, and he quickly turned around and sat down hard in his seat.

"I'm glad you said something," Fami told Seth. "He was kicking my seat too. We're never going to get any sleep. Could you feel it, Sadie?"

"No," she answered. "I was too busy *sleeping!*"

"I wish I could sleep," Seth said, covering the beginnings of a yawn.

"Me too," Fami echoed. "What time is it anyway?"

"London time or São Paulo time?" Seth asked.

"I don't know," he said. "Never mind."

"It's time to sleep, that's what time it is," Sadie said, this time shoving earplugs into her ears. "Wake me up when we get there." Her voice was unusually loud because of the earplugs, and it made Seth and Fami laugh.

"What?" Sadie said.

"Nothing," Seth said, still snickering. "I just hope you don't talk in your sleep."

* * *

The three kids thought they'd never get to Brazil. They were so sick of sitting in the cramped seats on the airplane, they decided to walk around the cabin a little and stretch their legs. The little boy behind them stuck his tongue out at Seth as he walked by, and Seth refrained from returning the gesture. The kid had finally fallen asleep during the flight, giving them at least two hours of peace and quiet. But as soon as the sun came up and someone raised the blind on their window, he was awake again, full of energy. Seth wondered if the little boy played soccer since all he did was kick his feet when he was sitting in his seat or run around the cabin driving the rest of the passengers crazy.

Sadie stayed by Fami to help him in case he needed any assistance. His glasses didn't work well inside the plane, so he was back to being sightless.

They had to stop in the aisle and wait for a man to pass by. "Excuse me, kids," he said with a

British accent. "Stretching your legs a bit?" The man had bleached blond hair, which he wore in gelled spikes. He wore small-framed, wire-rimmed glasses, and his jeans were torn and frayed in places. He had on a T-shirt that said *Tower of London Records* on it.

Sadie looked at him in awe, wondering if he were a rock star or something. "Uh, yeah," she stammered.

"Don't blame you there. I'm a bit stiff myself." He looked at Fami, then back at her. "Well, have a nice flight, then."

Just then, they hit some turbulence and the plane shook. All of them grabbed onto the seats closest to them and hung on. Fami's face went white.

"Hey there, mate," the British man said to Fami. "Just a bit of turbulence. Nothing to worry about."

Fami smiled bravely, and Sadie appreciated the man's reassuring words. Even she was a little nervous to have the plane shimmying like it was. After a few moments, things seemed to calm down.

"All's well then," the British man said, giving them a thumbs-up.

"Guess we'd better get back to our seats while we can," Fami suggested.

Sadie nodded but didn't respond.

The man went back to his seat as Sadie guided Fami down the aisle. "What was that all about?" Fami asked her.

"I'm not sure, but I think that guy we just talked to is a rock star or something."

"Really?" Fami said.

"I don't recognize him. He just looks like he's famous."

Many of the passengers still attempted to sleep, but all of them looked uncomfortable, curled up and twisted in their seats, and the turbulence wasn't making it any easier.

"Watch out for that lady's foot on your left," Sadie said. The sleeping woman was sprawled out all over her seat and the aisle.

Fami negotiated around her with a little help from Sadie. They were almost back to their seats and hoping that the flight attendants were going to give them some breakfast soon when Sadie looked up and saw a dark-skinned man with long, stringy hair looking intensely at Fami.

Sadie couldn't help feeling uncomfortable and creeped out having the man staring at them.

"Our seats are right here," Sadie said quickly, giving Fami a push from behind to get him to hurry and sit down.

"Ow," he exclaimed. "Okay, I got it."

They sat down and Fami said, "Geez, Sadie."

"I'm sorry, I didn't mean to jab you so hard. It's just that this man was watching us, and he seemed a little creepy," she explained.

"Noooo," Seth said, clapping his hand onto his forehead with disbelief. "Not again. I swear I'll jump out of this airplane right now. Can't we go anywhere without someone coming after us?"

"Hey, we've had spy training; we can handle it," Fami said, patting the black leather case that contained their state-of-the-art spy gadgets beneath his seat.

Sadie knew he was joking, but the joke wasn't funny. They'd run for their lives too many times. She didn't want to do it again. In fact, she wished her life were dull and boring and . . . safe!

"Yeah, you're right," Seth said. "Bring it on!" He and Fami high-fived in the air, then did some ridiculous handshake that went on for nearly a minute.

"Are you two done?" Sadie said with annoyance. "I'm serious. This man is really creepy."

"Here." Seth slid on his sunglasses. "I'll take a look. Where is he?"

"Straight back and to the right."

"What does he look like?"

"You'll know him when you see him," Sadie told her brother. "He's got long, stringy black hair and dark skin. Really beady eyes."

"What are beady eyes?"

"You know, creepy."

"Like evil creepy or scary creepy?"

"Just creepy creepy. I can't explain it."

"Okay, okay. Hey, wait just a minute. I think I see him." He concentrated on the image inside his glasses. There, just like Sadie had described, was a strange man with dark skin, black stringy hair, and eyes that the word *beady* described perfectly. And he was looking directly at Seth. Almost like he knew Seth was looking at him.

Seth dropped down hard in his seat.

"What happened? Did you see him?" Sadie asked.

"Yeah, he's back there all right."

"And?"

"He is kind of creepy in a mysterious sort of way."

"What do you mean?"

"It was like he knew."

"Knew what?"

"Knew I was looking at him."

Fami's expression grew worried. "That's very creepy. And you all remember what happened the last time a creepy man followed us around."

"Yeah," Seth said. "But he's not creepy evil, like before. He's creepy mysterious."

"Creepy is creepy," Sadie said.

"Wait a second," Fami said. "Let's not over-react. My dad probably had everyone on this plane checked out before we even got on board. I'm sure we're fine."

"I hope so," Sadie said.

"I smell food," Seth announced scanning the cabin for the source of his delight. "Yes!" He pumped the air with his fist. "Breakfast!"

Soon carts rolled down the aisles, and the attendants handed out little trays of food to each passenger. Sadie turned her attention to the food, realizing that she was actually hungry too.

"Isn't it amazing how food can make you forget just about everything?" Seth said with his mouth full. "You probably even forgot about your fear of flying," he said to Fami.

"It's not a fear of flying I have," Fami told him. "It's a fear of crashing."

Sadie realized that trading seats with Fami probably wasn't a good idea. Seth was just an annoyance to her, but he could probably get Fami freaked out about them landing in the ocean and dying on impact or being eaten by sharks, an occurrence Seth seemed to prefer if he were going to die.

Chapter 5

BAD LUCK

"Seth, look," Sadie said, nudging her brother. "The creepy man is coming our way."

They were inside the terminal, waiting for their luggage at the baggage claim. The man had his carry-on luggage in one hand and was hurrying to catch up with a large bag. He couldn't reach his bag in time, so he gave up trying until it came around again. He stood right next to them and plopped the bags in his hands down on the ground.

Seth had been looking over the rest of their flight plans to see if meals were provided and was pleased to see a meal being served on their way to Porto Alegre, their next destination. Satisfied, he folded the itinerary and tucked it into his back pocket, then watched the carousel for their luggage. Sadie already had her suitcase, but Seth and Fami still didn't have theirs.

Looking out of the corner of his eye at the man, who was standing next to Fami, Seth noticed that he wasn't much taller than Fami. He had markings, like tattoos, on his arms. His clothes were nothing out of the ordinary—flip-flops, denim shorts, and a loose, white T-shirt. But it was the tattoos that caught Seth's curiosity. They were strange black designs and markings, not typical tattoos of dragons, skulls, and hearts with someone's name inside. What was this man up to? And why did they keep bumping into him?

"Seth," Sadie exclaimed, "there's Fami's suitcase."

Seth quickly snapped out of his trance and deftly reached out to grab the handle of Fami's suitcase. He pulled it from the carousel and deposited it on the floor next to him.

"Thanks," Fami said, pulling up the handle so he could roll the luggage.

Seth glanced over at the man again, and their gazes connected, sending a shiver up his spine. The man looked directly at him.

Diverting his gaze to the carousel, Seth saw that his bag had rounded the corner and was coming his way. He stepped up, grabbed his suitcase, and deposited it onto the floor. He turned to join Fami and Sadie and noticed the tattooed man walking away. "Let's go find your parents," he said to Fami. "Do you want me to take the carry-on?"

"Sure," Fami said, reaching for his black leather bag.

"Here," Seth said, picking up and handing the bag to Fami. It had somehow gotten pushed off to the side.

Once they got all their luggage and hooked up with Fami's parents, they were ready to find out the details on Seth and Sadie's parents' arrival.

"The arrival board is on the second floor," Rob told them. "We'll need to go up the escalator. Make sure you kids stay close and keep an eye on your luggage."

Seth thought about how lucky they were they hadn't lost their spy gadget case. He'd rather lose all their luggage than the spy gadgets.

The airport seemed like any regular airport, busy and crowded. All around them, people spoke Portuguese at a rapid pace. Seth and Sadie looked at each other at one point and shook their heads. There was no way they would ever consider moving here. German had been hard enough, but this language sounded twice as hard.

"What time do Mom and Dad get here?" Sadie asked Fami's parents.

"Their plane should arrive in just a little over an hour, but we'll check to see if it's on time," Rob said.

"If we have time," Peredot said privately to Sadie, "maybe you and I can sneak off and do some shopping. Did you bring a pair of rubber flip-flops with you?"

"No," Sadie answered. "Was I supposed to?"

"You don't want to go barefoot while you are here, even in the shower. Each of you should have a pair of flip-flops to protect your feet from fungus and disease."

Sadie shuddered at the thought. "I don't have anything like that in my suitcase. It was chilly in London."

"The stores here will have what we need," Peredot assured her.

They found the arrival board and noticed that the Fletchers' plane was right on time, giving them an hour to kill.

"I'm starving," Seth said.

"You know, I'm a little hungry myself," Rob said. "How about you, son?"

"Sure," Fami said. "What do they have here?"

"I don't know. Let's go see," his father answered.

"Are you hungry, Sadie?" Peredot asked.

"Not really."

"Rob, since neither Sadie nor I are hungry, why don't you take the boys and go get some food. We'll see what we can find in the shops. I'm guessing you boys don't have flip-flops either."

The two boys shook their heads.

"Then it's settled," Peredot said. "Sadie and I will find flip-flops and meet you back here in half an hour."

"Sounds like a plan," Rob said. "You two stick together."

"We will, honey," she replied, giving her husband a quick kiss good-bye. "Come on, my dear," Peredot said to Sadie. "We can pick up a snack for later."

Peredot and Sadie located a gift shop where they found a huge assortment of flip-flops and an assortment of snacks.

Sadie also saw a display of bright yellow Brazil T-shirts trimmed with green and blue, the colors in the Brazilian flag. In bins below the T-shirt display were stacks of neatly folded shirts in different sizes. She crouched down, trying to locate an extra small in the style she wanted. Rob had explained the money system to the kids and had told them that approximately three Brazilian Reais equaled one American dollar. If that were true, the T-shirts were only five dollars each.

She had to go through the entire stack before she finally found the size she needed. She then stood up and looked around but couldn't see Peredot anywhere. Sadie's heart skipped a beat. She circled inside the store, hoping to find Fami's mom, but the store was empty. Wondering if Peredot had stepped outside of the store for a moment, Sadie rushed through the doors to look for her, setting off an alarm.

Sadie froze.

The woman from the store raced over to her, firing off Portuguese words like bullets from a machine gun. She pulled Sadie back into the store by her arm.

"I'm sorry. I'm looking for my friend," Sadie said as tears stung her eyes.

The woman continued talking as a security guard joined them.

"Do you speak English?" Sadie said to him. "I didn't mean to take the shirt. I was looking for the woman who came into the store with me."

"The woman?" the guard said.

"Yes, she bought three pair of flip-flops and chips and candy."

"Fleep-flops?" he attempted to say.

"Yes, you know," Sadie glanced around and saw the rack of shoes. "Flip-flops."

The man looked at her, his face still filled with confusion.

"Please," Sadie said. "You have to understand. I wasn't trying to steal the shirt. I lost my friend. I just wanted to look outside to see where she was."

Another woman from a back room joined them. Sadie supposed it was a manager or maybe even the storeowner.

The three adults discussed something in a slur of Portuguese, while Sadie's head reeled.

"Could I be of assistance?" a man's voice said. "I speak Portuguese."

Sadie turned to see the rock star from the airplane. Relief flooded over her. "Oh, could you please? They think I tried to steal this T-shirt, but I just ran to look for my friend. I think she left without me."

"Don't worry, little lady, I'll see what I can do."

The man approached the store manager and launched into an explanation, pointing occasionally at Sadie, then at the shirt, then shrugging. The woman who had come from the back gave a nod and a kind smile to Sadie.

The man turned back to Sadie. "She remembers your friend and remembered her leaving in a big hurry."

Sadie handed the shirt to the woman, then turned to the man. "Could you please tell her I'm sorry I caused any trouble?"

"Tell you what," he said, pulling out his wallet. "I'd like to get this shirt for you. That way you can have good memories instead of bad ones."

"Oh no, that's okay," she said.

"Please, I insist," the man said.

"Better let him do it, miss," his friend, a shorter man with shoulder-length hair and rectangle-lensed glasses, said. "Once he makes up his mind, there's no talking him out of it."

The man handed the woman some money, and she quickly rang up the shirt and slid it into a plastic bag. He handed the bag to Sadie. "There you go. Let's go find your friends now."

They walked out of the store and were headed for the escalator when Peredot came riding down the other side. "Sadie! There you are. I was so worried. Wait right there."

Peredot ran down the steps of the escalator and grabbed Sadie in a crushing hug.

"But you left *me* at the store," Sadie said when Peredot let go.

"What do you mean?" Peredot said. "Right after I purchased the flip-flops, I turned and you were nowhere to be seen. I stepped outside, and a man who spoke English asked me if I needed help. I told him I was looking for you, and he said he'd seen you on your way to the escalator."

"But I never left the store," Sadie insisted. "Who was the man?"

Peredot's forehead wrinkled with concern. "I don't know." She reached out and took Sadie's hand. "I think we'd better go find Rob and the boys. Thank you, Mr. . . ."

"Tyler. Thadeus Tyler. You might know me as Double T. I'm a rapper from Great Britain."

"I knew it," Sadie exclaimed. "I knew you were a rock star."

"Rapper," Double T corrected with a smile. "I haven't made it across Europe and into the

U.S. yet, but I go on tour this fall. Maybe I'll come to your city."

"We live in—"

"That would be nice, Mr. T. We'll watch for you," Peredot said quickly, cutting off Sadie's reply.

"Just call me Thad. That's what my friends call me."

"Where is your friend?" Sadie asked, realizing that the other man wasn't with them.

"Don't know. Maybe he got a phone call. He's my assistant, and I think he spends more time on the phone than off."

"Well, Thad, we appreciate your help and want to wish you luck. We really need to go now," Peredot interjected.

"Thanks for helping me," Sadie told him.

"My pleasure. Would you like an autograph before you go?" he offered.

"Are you kidding?" Sadie said. "Of course I would."

"How about I sign your shirt," he suggested. "Autographs are my favorite part of being famous."

Sadie snatched the shirt out of the bag and handed it to him with her camera pen, the only one she had available.

He clicked the pen and tried to write, but nothing happened. Sadie didn't tell him that he'd just taken a picture of himself.

"Here," she said, pushing another button to activate the pen's writing function. "Sorry, it doesn't work very well."

"No problem," he said, then he scrawled, *To my number 1 fan,* and signed it, *Double T.* He handed her the pen, then checked the shirt to make sure the autograph was to his liking. Satisfied, he handed it back to Sadie. "There you go, luv. That's a one of a kind."

"Thanks, Thad." She wished she had her regular camera with her to take a picture, but she didn't. The camera-pen shot would have to do.

Peredot and Sadie watched him leave, then Peredot said, "We really do need to hurry. The boys should be done eating by now."

Sadie looked at her shirt. This trip that had seemed like such a downer was suddenly exciting. She couldn't wait to show Seth her shirt.

Chapter 6

CREEPY MAN

"I bet he's not even a real rap star," Seth said as they waited for their parents to disembark. "He's probably one of those wannabes that stands on street corners and stuff and has people throw money into a hat."

"You're just jealous because Double T didn't buy you a shirt and autograph it."

"More like ruined it," Seth said. "His autograph looks like scribbling. No one's even going to know whose name is on it because he's not even famous."

"Your mom and dad should be coming any minute," Rob said. "Their plane landed ten minutes ago."

Seth continually scanned the stream of passengers for his parents, but still they didn't come.

"Maybe they want to be the last ones off," Fami suggested. "You know, dramatic effect."

"Maybe," Seth said. He couldn't wait to tell his dad all about the spy training and the things he'd learned.

"I don't understand," Rob said. "This was their flight. I'm sure of it."

"Maybe they missed their flight," Peredot offered.

"Wouldn't they call if they had?" Rob asked.

"Why don't you call them and see what happened?"

He placed the call, but there was no answer.

"Are we sure this is their flight?" Peredot asked her husband.

"I'll go check and see," Rob answered, walking to the Varig Airlines counter.

Seth watched Fami's dad anxiously. With their luck, anything could have happened to his parents.

"Planes get delayed all the time and people miss their connecting flights," Peredot told the children. "I'm sure nothing bad has happened."

Seth nodded woodenly, like he understood, but in his heart, he felt something was wrong. He couldn't put his finger on it, but something just didn't feel right.

"Here he comes," Sadie exclaimed.

"Well," Rob said, with a shake of his head, "the flight they were on out of Frankfurt didn't make the connection in Rome. There's been some sort of delay, mechanical they think, and your parents probably won't even make it to São Paulo tonight."

"Oh, man. Now what are we going to do?" Seth said. He was feeling grumpy and tired and not in the mood to hang around an airport for two days.

"Let me make a few calls," Rob said. "I'll track down your father and see what he wants us to do. We have an appointment with Luciano tomorrow. He's leaving for Argentina soon, and I hate to come all this way and not meet with him. I'll be right back."

"I need to use the restroom," Peredot told them. "You kids stay put. I'll be right back."

Fami muttered, "Soybeans," under his breath as his parents walked away. "I still can't believe it."

"Tell me about it," Seth said. "Do our parents not care that we have the most abnormal lives of anyone we know?"

"No kidding," Fami agreed. "I'd give anything for our dads to have regular jobs so we could go to a regular school, complain about having too much homework, and hang out with friends on weekends."

The children sprawled out on the hard plastic chairs and tried to catch a few winks. Seth had never been so tired in his life. His arms felt as though they were made of lead. His head was thick and groggy.

It seemed like only sixty seconds had gone by when Rob was back with some news.

"Honey, what is it?" Peredot said when her husband approached.

Seth fought through the fog in his brain and forced his eyes to open.

"They had to make an emergency landing in Italy. But they're fine," Rob explained.

"Emergency landing?" Seth asked. "What kind of emergency?"

"Well . . . you see . . ." Rob shut his eyes for a moment, as if gathering the strength to give them the news. "There was a bomb scare. Everyone's fine," he quickly assured them. "Three men were arrested."

"Were the three men—" Sadie started.

"Part of Bachmann's group? We don't know at this point, but there's an investigation."

Seth and Sadie sat in stunned silence. Someone had tried to blow up their parents' plane. The thought terrified them.

"Everything's fine now," Rob assured them. "The men each smuggled pieces of an explosive device onto the airplane. They were attempting to assemble it in the bathroom during the flight. Your father thought they were acting peculiar, and his suspicions were true."

"Can we talk to them?" Sadie asked, missing her parents more now than ever.

"Your father needed to make some calls, but he said he'd call right back. They are anxious to talk to you kids also. And," he looked at the three children directly as he continued, "he wants us to go on to Santa Maria without them. They're going to try and charter a plane so they can fly directly to us."

"The Lord was keeping an eye on them," Peredot told the children. "I have no doubt of that."

"That's exactly what they said. Now, I need to check on our flight to Porto Alegre. We'll get a rental car there and drive to Santa Maria."

"Is that where Luciano's place is?" Fami asked.

"It's near Santa Maria. He's meeting us there so he can take us to his farm."

"If anyone needs to use the restroom, you'd better do it now," Peredot told the children. "I'll wait right outside for you. Remember not to flush the toilet paper."

"What?" Seth exclaimed. "Are you kidding?"

"You might as well get in the habit of it now. They don't like you to flush the paper here. And you already know to not—"

"—drink the water," the kids said in unison.

"Just making sure. Now, hurry and use the restroom before your father gets back."

After washing her hands, Sadie hurried from the restroom, anxious to talk to her parents and find out when they would finally all be together again. Even though Fami's parents were wonderful, she'd still feel better when her own parents were with them.

She rushed through the door and stopped dead in her tracks, then took one step back. Her breath caught in her throat. With a gasp, she looked straight into the eyes of the creepy man from the airplane. His dark eyes were mere slits, and his long, stringy hair made him look wild and freaky.

Just then, Seth and Fami's voices preceded them, and a second later they stepped through the door of the men's room. "Hey, Sadie," Seth said, looking curiously at her, then at the wild, creepy man.

"I waited . . . for you," she managed to say as nonchalantly as she could, but remaining calm was difficult when she noticed that the man was carrying a black leather bag that looked exactly like their bag.

"Uh, thanks," Seth said, quickly catching on that something weird was going on.

The man looked at all three of them, but particularly at Fami.

"Can we go now?" Fami said, wondering why they were stopping.

"Sure," Seth said, taking his friend's arm and stepping out of the man's way.

"Uh, wait," Sadie said, trying to draw attention to the bag. "You didn't forget anything in the rest-room did you? Like your carry-on or anything?"

Seth's eyebrows narrowed. "Uh, no," he said.

She tried to divert her eyes in the direction of the man's bag, but Seth wasn't catching on.

"Kids!" Peredot called to them. "You need to hurry. The plane is boarding."

"Come on," Seth said.

"But—"

"We gotta go," Seth said through gritted teeth.

The three kids rushed over to Fami's mom, who had their bags ready for them so they could run to their gate. Sadie plowed through all their luggage and carry-on bags until she found what she was looking for. "Whew! I was so scared there for a minute."

"What?" Seth demanded.

"That man. The one from the plane," she explained. "He was carrying a bag just like ours. For a minute, I wondered if maybe he'd taken it."

"I'm sorry, children, but Rob is waiting. We have to run. Do we have everything, then?" Peredot asked.

"Got it," Seth answered. He helped Fami with his backpack and the black carry-on bag.

Without another minute to spare, the three kids followed Peredot through the São Paulo airport to the gate. They would board a plane that would take them to the very bottom of Brazil, into the heart of the gaúcho country, where agriculture and cattle were the primary resources. And, of course, soybeans.

* * *

"We'll try your parents again in a few minutes," Rob told Seth and Sadie as they all walked to the car rental booth. "They're anxious to talk to you."

They'd tried to call when they arrived in Porto Alegre, an hour and a half flight from São Paulo, but there had been no answer. Sadie tried hard not to let her imagination run away with her, but she couldn't help it. They'd had so many freaky things happen to them they never knew what to expect anymore.

It took some time to get the car arranged, but soon they were loading their luggage into the back of a small minivan parked out in front of the airport terminal.

It felt good to be outside, even though the air was hot and humid. Porto Alegre was a large, thriving city on the southeast coast of Brazil. Palms and other tropical greenery created a lovely backdrop for the brightly colored homes that dotted the rolling hills.

"How far is the drive to Santa Maria, Dad?" Fami asked.

"About four hours."

"What?" Fami exclaimed as a yawn took over. "You're serious?"

"We're all tired, son, but we're almost there. We'll stop and get some food on the way."

"Food?" Seth perked up. "I'm so hungry I'll eat anything."

"The food here in the south is very good," Rob said, "but be prepared for things to be a little different. Everyone pile in. It's time to hit the road."

Fami and Seth climbed in first, claiming the backseat of the minivan all for themselves. Sadie was the last one to get in. She pulled the door shut and looked out the window at the airport as they drove away. Then something caught her eye. A face in the crowd. In a blink, it was gone.

She couldn't be sure it was the tattooed man from the São Paulo airport—most of the Brazilians had the same bronze-colored skin and black hair. Besides, how could the creepy man have followed them to Porto Alegre? Wouldn't she have seen him on the plane?

It didn't make sense, and it didn't matter any-more anyway. They were pulling onto the busy on-ramp and blending into the thousands of cars barreling at high speeds along the freeway. Even if he were trying to follow them, it would be impossible now.

* * *

"I think I'm going to explode," Seth said, leaning back in his chair and pushing his plate away from him.

"You know, Seth," Rob said, "I think you just set a new record for 'all-you-can-eat.' They might just have to raise their prices to cover all the food you ate."

"I can't help it," Seth said. "Everything was so good. Well, almost everything." He shuddered when he thought about the cow brain he'd tasted. He'd been fine until they told him what he'd been eating. But all the barbecued meats were better than anything he'd ever eaten. The waiter kept coming by with a dozen varieties of chicken and beef and pork, seasoned with flavors that were out of this world. He felt like he'd died and gone to heaven. Even more amazing was that the meal cost less per person than a McDonald's Happy Meal back in America.

"If everybody's full, we'd better get going. We still have a few hours left, and Luciano said it's not wise to drive in the dark."

"Why not, Dad?" Fami asked.

"Mainly because we aren't familiar with the roads, and it will be harder to watch for the landmarks and road signs. Also, he said there are a lot of pedestrians on the road, even at night. We need to be very careful."

"Why are people walking on the highways?"

"Not very many people own cars, so they either walk or drive a horse and buggy, like you've seen."

"It seems kind of dangerous for horses and buggies to be on the same road as cars," Seth remarked.

"It is dangerous, but they are as common as automobiles in this area."

The countryside through which they traveled was lush and green and very beautiful. They saw a group of ostriches in a field and were amazed to hear that they were raised to be eaten in Brazil, just like chicken or beef.

"Rob, look out!" Peredot hollered. A small bird slammed into the windshield with an enormous thud, then tumbled onto the side of the road.

"What happened?" Fami exclaimed.

"We just killed a bird," Seth said.

"The man at the rental car place warned me about the birds," Rob said. "I didn't even see that one coming. He just appeared out of—"

"Rob, look out!"

Rob suddenly slammed on the brakes again, just in time to miss a horse and buggy pulling onto the street. The wheels skidded on the pavement, and the back end of the car swung to the right and plowed into a road sign with a picture of a horse and buggy on it, knocking it over with a loud crash.

When the car came to an abrupt stop, all the passengers sat in stunned silence until the whinny of a horse broke the stillness.

"Everyone okay?" Rob asked. "Honey?"

"I'm fine," Peredot said. "Just a little shook up. Kids?"

"I hit my head, but I'm okay," Seth said.

"I'm fine, Mom."

"Me too," Sadie added.

A tap on his window brought Rob's head around with a snap. The man who'd been riding the horse peered inside at the passengers. Rob rolled down the window, and the man released a string of Portuguese words.

"He's asked if we're okay, and he's also angry at me for almost hitting his horse," Rob translated. He replied to the man, who nodded and answered back with quick, angry words.

The man wore puffy legged pants tucked into tall leather boots and a five-inch-wide belt with an enormous buckle in the front. Tucked into the belt in the back was a large, leather-sheathed knife. Just then, the man reached into his pocket and pulled out a cell phone. He placed a call, then nodded and gestured with his hands as he appeared to explain the crash.

"I need to call Luciano and tell him we're going to be a little late," Rob said, pulling out his own phone.

Peredot and the kids decided to wait outside underneath a tree. Without the air conditioner running, the car had grown extremely hot. After a few minutes, a car approached from the opposite direction. As it drew nearer, it became obvious that it was a local highway patrolman. The officer pulled off the side of the road and walked cautiously toward them. To everyone's horror, he had his handgun raised and was aiming right at them.

Chapter 7

Follow the Leader

"Everyone stay calm," Rob said. "Let me handle this."

The officer stopped ten feet from the van passengers and eyed them warily. Upon seeing the three kids, he lowered his pistol and seemed to relax. He cautiously approached, his gaze slipping to the van, then to the passengers. "You are tourists?"

"Yes," Rob said.

The man with the buggy stepped up and said something to the officer, who nodded and looked at Rob.

"You must come with me."

"Where?" Rob said. "I can't just leave my family here."

"The speed limit here is forty kilometers per hour. That man said you were doing twice that amount."

"I wasn't speeding, officer. In fact, I was probably going under the speed limit because we'd just hit a bird and I was being very careful."

The officer's brow narrowed with doubt.

"We can show you the bird," Seth piped up. "I know right where it landed. It's just over there, by that power pole."

The officer looked at each of them, then said, "You show me this bird, and maybe we can work something out."

Rob gave Seth a pat on his back and let the boy lead the way.

The man from the buggy followed them, apparently continuing to argue his case against them.

Seth led to where the bird had landed, its lifeless body sprawled in the dirt.

They all squatted down around the bird and stared at it for a moment. Seth reached out to touch its feathers, and the officer said, "Wait!"

Seth jerked his hand back in fright.

"Let me see your hand again," the officer said.

Slowly, Seth extended his arm and spread out his fingers, palm up.

"Turn your hand over," the officer instructed.

Following the command, Seth turned over his hand, waiting for the officer to clap a pair of handcuffs onto his wrist. Instead, the officer looked at the ring Seth had on his middle finger.

"*C-T-R,*" the officer said.

Seth looked up at him.

"You are Mormon?"

Seth nodded.

The officer looked at the ring again, then said, "So am I."

Seth and Rob caught each other's gaze and smiled with relief.

They all stood up, and the officer talked to the man with the buggy. The man was clearly agitated, but the officer spoke again with a strong tone that meant business, and the man turned and walked back to his rig, climbed inside, and clip-clopped on down the highway.

"Do you still need us to come with you?" Rob asked him.

"Not at all. I believe what you say. The bird is also proof that you are telling the truth."

"Thank you, Officer . . ." Rob looked at the man's name tag, ". . . Sousa. We appreciate your kindness."

"I am recent convert to the Church," Officer Sousa said. "The missionaries gave me a CTR ring when I was baptized, but I lost it."

Seth didn't waste a second pulling the ring off his finger. "You can have mine."

"Oh, no, that wouldn't be right."

"Sure it would," Seth said. "I can get another one anytime. I want you to have it."

Officer Sousa smiled. "Thank you. I am very happy to have it." He took the ring from Seth and smiled as he slid it onto several different fingers before leaving it on his pinky finger. "I like it very much."

"We're sorry about the road sign," Rob said as they approached the others.

"No problem."

"Well, if that's all, we need to be on our way," Rob said to their new friend. "We are heading the right direction toward Santa Maria, aren't we?"

"Yes, this road takes you straight to Santa Maria."

Rob nodded. "Thanks, again."

The officer touched the brim of his hat in farewell, just as a loud voice came over his two-way radio. He rushed to his car to respond as the five travelers crawled back into their van, hoping that it still ran after the collision.

Rob inserted the key into the ignition and was about to start the van when a loud knocking came at his window.

"Yes, Officer?" he asked.

"I'm sorry, but I'm going to have to ask you to come with me to the station. There's been a bulletin put out for your arrest."

"What?" Rob exclaimed.

"All of you will need to come with me." The officer rested his hand on the pistol at his hip, indicating he didn't want any resistance.

"We'd better do as the man says," Rob told them.

* * *

"What do you mean we stole a briefcase from a man in the São Paulo airport? You can search our van. We have nothing of the sort with us," Rob explained.

"The man claims that he was standing next to your children at the baggage claim, and the next thing he knew, his briefcase was gone and so were your children," the chief officer explained. "He was left with a decoy that looks very similar to his but cannot be opened."

"A decoy. I don't believe this," Rob exclaimed.

"This man's briefcase contained top-secret information. The man said your children had been eyeing him on the plane and at the airport. He was afraid something was going on."

"Wait!" Sadie piped up as a thought crossed her mind. "Creepy man. It has to be."

"We didn't steal his briefcase!" Seth said in their defense.

"Maybe it's a setup," Sadie replied. "Sir," she asked the officer in charge, "did the man describe his briefcase to you?"

"Yes, of course."

"Is it black leather, five inches thick, eighteen inches long, and twelve inches high?"

"Yes, that's it."

Sadie looked at Fami and Seth. "We didn't take his briefcase. I think he stole our briefcase and is setting *us* up!"

"Oh no," Fami exclaimed. "We've got to get our briefcase back!"

"Children, what are you talking about?" Rob asked them.

"Sir," Sadie addressed the man, "the two briefcases may be similar, but our bag has a unique identifying mark."

"And what is that?"

"There's a big round mustard stain on the bottom right-hand corner," Sadie told him.

"Well, there's one way to get to the bottom of this," the police chief said. "Bring him in."

All three children gasped.

"Creepy man is here?" Sadie whispered, getting chills. She stepped back closer to her brother and Fami.

"What do you think this guy is up to?" Seth whispered as the door opened.

"I don't know," Fami answered, "but we need our stuff back."

One of the officers walked in, followed by the long-haired, creepy man carrying the black briefcase—*their* black briefcase.

"That's it!" Sadie blurted out. "That's our leather case."

The man glared at her, and she quickly shrank back.

Peredot stepped over to the children and put a protective arm around them.

"Mr. Mendoza, can you identify these children?" the chief asked the man.

"Yes," he said with a thick Brazilian accent. "These are the children who stole my briefcase."

"What?" Seth erupted.

"Seth, calm down. We'll get to the bottom of this," Rob told him.

"This is a setup," Sadie said under her breath.

"On the airplane and at the baggage claim, these children were watching me," Mr. Mendoza explained. "I could tell they were up to something. I didn't realize until it was too late that they had switched briefcases with me."

Seth struggled with the urge to defend themselves, but Rob gave him a warning look to keep his mouth closed and wait.

"Luckily, I noticed all of them at Gate Two." He gestured toward them. "I knew that plane went to Porto Alegre, and I figured they would have to rent a car, so I was able to track them down and catch the next plane to Porto Alegre."

The chief nodded as he listened to the story.

"The contents of my briefcase are vital to the future of my people. I must guard it with my life."

"Well, the stuff in our briefcase is important to us too!" Seth blurted out, then realized he'd disobeyed Fami's father. "Sorry."

"Sir," the LDS officer spoke up, "I believe this is not a theft, but an unfortunate mix-up. The bags do look identical."

"It was very hectic at the baggage claim too," Sadie told the officer. "He must have set his bag next to ours, and when we got all our luggage, we accidentally took his instead of ours. But we didn't steal it. We want our own briefcase. It's got some very important equipment in it that we need."

"Yeah," Seth said. "How do we know he wasn't trying to steal *our* briefcase?"

"I don't think he would've chased after us all this way if he'd stolen our briefcase," Fami told him.

"True." Seth felt his face redden.

The chief stood up and walked around his desk. "All right. What if we get a positive identification on each briefcase, make sure they are returned to the rightful owners, and send you both on your way? Would that make everyone happy?"

Mr. Mendoza looked at the kids and Mr. and Mrs. Laningham and thought for a moment, then said, "Yes."

"Very well, then. Mr. Mendoza, could you describe your briefcase and the contents for us? We also need it opened."

He gave them the key to unlock the case. "You will find plant samples and signed laboratory documents."

"What are these samples for, Mr. Mendoza?" the chief asked.

Mr. Mendoza glanced around the room, as if trying to decide how much information he could divulge, then said, "I am a member of the Macuxi tribe. We live in the jungle near Iguassu Falls on the border near Paraguay. For hundreds of years, my people have used the plants and trees in our jungle to cure everything from broken bones and injuries to infections and cancers. We are able to cure almost any affliction. I am returning from a laboratory in Florida that is testing the medicinal properties of these plants. If they prove effective, which I know they will, then we will be able to grow and harvest these plants to make money for my people to live on, and we will also be able to preserve our jungle and rain forest."

"Is this the same area that has been having trouble with gold mining and illegal loggers?" the police chief asked.

"Yes. Ever since they discovered gold on our land, white men have tried to take our land so they can mine the gold. There are also men cutting down our trees and ruining our jungle. They will destroy the rain forest. Our people and all of the animals that live there will die."

The chief nodded. "This has been a very difficult situation for the government," he explained to the Laninghams and the children. "The natives have been given this land by the government. It is theirs to inhabit and protect. These miners have no right to mine their gold, but the government is having a hard time stopping them."

"So, it's up to us," Mr. Mendoza said. "But we are no match for these men who are jungle commandos. They drive around in jeeps with M16 assault rifles. They have killed many of my people and those of other villages. It is a very bad situation for us. If we can get the government to recognize the medicinal value of our plants and trees, they will work harder to preserve our land and help us. Because I speak English and went to a university in America, I have been chosen to represent my people. It is up to me to do all I can to save them and our land."

As Sadie listened to the man tell of the struggles of his people, she noticed a change in his appearance or at least her perception of him. He was no longer a creepy man, but a warrior, fighting for his rights. A man trying to save his land and his people.

"Mr. Mendoza," Rob said, "I want to apologize for this inconvenience to you, having to come all this way for your briefcase."

Mr. Mendoza lowered his head in thanks. "Our future lies inside that case," he said. "I never should have put it down, but I needed to so I could get my luggage. I am sorry for accusing you of stealing it."

"It's understandable," Rob said. "Unfortunate, but understandable."

"Isn't there anything we can do to help these people?" Peredot asked the chief and Rob. "They're under attack. I've read about this situation in your jungle. I saw the article when I was doing some research about Brazil on the internet."

"It is out of my hands," the chief said. "We have our own problems we must deal with."

She looked at her husband, who gave her a reassuring smile. "The least we can do is take Mr. Mendoza and get him a nice meal and a hotel room. I'd also like to pay for your flight home," Rob told the man.

"That would be very kind of you," Mr. Mendoza said. "I'm afraid that I am low on resources."

"Then by all means, we will take care of your expenses," Rob said. "Perhaps we can talk and find more ways we can help."

* * *

"So, Mr. Mendoza," Rob asked, "can you think of anything we can do to help you and your people?" They had stopped to talk in the lobby of the hotel where Mr. Mendoza would spend the night, then fly back to his home the next morning. The kids had found an ice cream store nearby and were happily enjoying delicious frozen treats as they listened to the conversation.

"Please, call me by my first name, Tiago."

"Okay, Tiago, but tell me—isn't your government doing anything to help your people?"

"Yes, they are almost finished building a dam that will help provide much-needed electricity to the area and clean water for us to drink. Right now, only a few villages, like mine, have electrical power. I have to use a satellite phone because we don't get cell phone service. But in a few months, when it is completed, our people will have these conveniences. Farmers in the surrounding areas can begin to grow crops that will help feed our people. Once again, we will prosper. This dam is very important to our people and the rain forest."

"That's good. I'm glad to hear the government is helping."

"Yes, but you see, the illegal miners and illegal logging companies are not happy about it. When the dam is fully functional, it will flood the area above the dam and cover the areas they are mining. They do not want this dam completed and are causing much trouble for us."

"I can see why. Those men don't care about preserving the rain forest. They just want their gold and the timber."

"Yes, at any cost, even the lives of the tribal people. This is why we are trying to get the attention of the medical community. If they recognize the worth of the plants on our land, greater efforts will be made by the government to protect it and even fund our efforts to grow and protect the plants that can help cure people of many diseases that cause so much sickness and death."

"What exactly are these medicines you have tested?" Rob asked.

"We believe we have one that will help grow healthy cells and prevent cancer from growing. In fact, it can also reverse some forms of cancer."

"That's amazing," Peredot said. "I'm stunned that we possibly could see a cure for cancer in the near future."

"We also have a fungus that will cure the common cold. Bronchitis, sinus infections, and even pneumonia could be wiped out with this."

"Perhaps we could contact people we know in the United States in the medical community who could help," Rob said.

"Yes, that would be good. We need help with research and funding. But we need to move quickly. The men wanting the gold and the timber are very aggressive and impatient. If they aren't stopped, we cannot continue our work, and we will lose our rain forest."

"The whole planet will suffer," Fami said.

"Yes," Tiago said, then he looked directly at Fami. "You might be interested to know that there is a tree that grows in our jungle called the faveiro tree. The leaves from this tree can strengthen blood vessels. It works as an anti-inflammatory, but the greatest use for it, we've found, is in aiding regeneration of nerve tissue and nerve endings."

"Are you saying that someone with nerve damage could take this medicine and the damage would be repaired?"

"Yes, that's exactly what I'm telling you," Tiago said. "One of the men in our village fell from a coconut tree. Landed on his back and couldn't move his arms or legs. After two weeks of, taking medicine made from faveiro leaves, he was back on his feet. Slowly he has gotten stronger, until now, today, he is perfectly fine."

Rob and Peredot exchanged glances.

"You still do not believe?"

"It's just that, well, such a remedy would be a medical breakthrough. A miracle drug."

"I know it happened, because I was the man who fell. We have been using these plants for many years." Then Tiago looked at Rob. "May I ask your son a question?"

"Of course," Rob answered.

Fami tilted his head toward Tiago's voice.

"You are not able to see, correct?"

"I can see contrast between dark and light," Fami answered. "Sometimes I can make out shapes and forms. And I've had a few experiences where I've actually had my sight return for a brief second or two."

"You were not born this way?"

"No," Peredot answered. "Fami was struck by lightning."

Tiago's forehead wrinkled as he pondered what she said, then he spoke. "You have survived lightning?"

"Actually both my husband and son were struck at the same time," Peredot told him. "That's how Fami lost his sight."

"And you, Rob?"

"Nothing like what my son has suffered," Rob answered.

Tiago nodded his head thoughtfully. "That is good." He then looked at Fami. "What would you say if I told you I could restore your sight?"

Fami's sightless eyes opened wide, along with his mouth, but no words came out.

"Tiago, please," Peredot said. "I don't want to get his hopes up."

"No," Tiago said, "it is true. The faveiro leaves can restore Fami's sight."

"We've already tried every—"

"Dad!" Fami interrupted. "Please, let him talk."

Rob looked at his son and gave a single nod. "All right, Tiago, why do you think these leaves can help my son?"

"Fami," Tiago said, not answering Rob's question, "you said you have had moments when your vision has been clear and you've been able to see?"

"Only for one or two seconds. It's almost like my eye is the lens of a camera, and it snaps a quick photo."

"I understand," Tiago said. "It all makes sense."

"What makes sense?" Peredot demanded, the concern in her face apparent.

"Our paths have crossed for a reason. We were brought together for this very purpose. I have something I can do for you. You have something you can do for me. We are supposed to help each other. We have been sent to alter each other's futures."

Chapter 8

A Change of Plans

Rob and Peredot exchanged glances, as did Seth and Sadie. Tiago was making a bold claim. A claim that a miracle could happen.

"The nerves in your eyes are letting you know they are alive and functioning. They just need a way to regenerate and reconnect. This is the main property of the faveiro leaf."

"Tiago, you talk like you really believe you can do this," Fami said.

"I do not believe I can do this," Tiago corrected. "I know I can."

Peredot reached for her husband's hand.

"If you came to the jungle with me, we could do this. We could bring back your sight."

Rob and Peredot looked at each other, their faces lined with concern but their eyes alive with hope.

"Dad, Mom," Fami said, "did you hear that? Did you?"

"Yes, son," Rob answered.

"He can do it. He said he could make my sight return," Fami exclaimed.

Seth and Sadie exchanged excited looks. As far as Seth was concerned, Fami had nothing to fear or lose. Still, it would be cruel to get his hopes up for nothing.

"Dad, I want to go with him. I want to go to the jungle," Fami begged. "Something tells me this is right."

Rob opened his mouth to speak, but then he quickly closed it and looked at his wife.

"What if he *can* do it?" she asked her husband.

"We need some time to think about this," Rob finally said. "And we can't forget the reason we came to Brazil in the first place. We have a very important appointment we have to keep before we can go anywhere else."

Tiago bowed his head in respect of their wishes. "Then I will return to my people and prepare to welcome you and your family to our village. I, too, have an important appointment to keep."

"Then we will keep you and your people in our prayers," Peredot said to him.

An expression of confusion crossed Tiago's face. "You would pray for us?"

"Yes, of course," she said. "We all will."

The children nodded as well as Rob.

He shut his eyes and scrunched his face as an obvious wave of emotion washed over him. Then, after the moment passed, Tiago swallowed hard and opened his eyes, dewy wet with tears. "I do not know how to thank you."

"If you can help our son, we will not know how to thank you," Rob said.

"But isn't that why we are here on this earth? To help each other?" Tiago asked.

* * *

They ended up staying in a hotel with Tiago, and after a good night's sleep, they said good-bye to him and continued the journey to Santa Maria.

"It's all settled. Your parents will be here the day after tomorrow so they can take a tour of the soybean farm and meet with Luciano before he leaves for Argentina with his family." Rob slipped his satellite phone into his shirt pocket and slowed down as the van neared a horse and buggy on the side of the road.

"Dad, how serious are you and Mr. Fletcher about this farm?" Fami asked.

"I don't know. We'll just have to see what it's like and what's involved. We aren't making any commitments yet. We haven't packed any boxes."

"We don't have anything to pack even if we do move," Sadie said.

"No kiddin'," Seth replied. "We're like . . . homeless!"

The word was sobering to both Sadie and Seth. They really were homeless. And all the clothes they had were the ones they had with them. Sadie thought about all her scrapbooks and pictures, books and jewelry and keepsakes. She thought of Seth's chemistry set, his science books, all the equipment for his magic tricks, his sports gear, computer, and the rest of his stuff. Was all of it gone?

"Rob," Seth spoke up after a while, "what do you think it's going to take to stop all of these attacks on our families?"

Rob contemplated Seth's question for a few moments. "Well, Seth, I guess that's what we're all wondering. But I know one way to stop them is to get the man at the top. If we get him, his whole empire will crumble."

"You mean Bachmann, Dad?"

"Yes, son. Constantine Bachmann is the driving force behind all of this. Even Skordos and his men would go away. They're just pawns in Bachmann's game."

"What about those men you testified against? Isn't that why he's after us?" Sadie asked.

"Yes, but those men alone can't sustain the attacks and the threats. Bachmann is the brains and the bucks behind the operations. Without him orchestrating every move his men make and putting up the money to pay for their expenses, these guys would be nothing."

"Sometimes I still can't believe that Frau Bachmann really turned on us. She was like a grandma to us," Sadie said.

"When it comes to money and power, some people will do just about anything," Rob explained.

"Yeah, look at the problems Tiago and his people are having because of people wanting money and power. I'm glad we're going to try and help them, Dad," Fami said. "Even if they can't make my sight return, they need our help."

* * *

"Did my mom and dad say anything about going to Iguassu Falls to see Tiago after we're done at Luciano's?" Seth asked.

"We didn't really get much time to talk about it," Rob told him. "I'm sure they'll be fine with the arrangement. It's a coincidence, but we'd actually talked about taking you kids to see the falls while we were in Brazil."

"The falls are quite an amazing sight," Peredot told them. "They are on the border of

Brazil and Argentina near Paraguay. There are anywhere between 150 and 300 waterfalls, depending on what time of year it is and how full the Iguassu River is."

"No kidding? Three hundred waterfalls?" Seth asked.

"It's one of the natural wonders of the world," Peredot told him.

"And Tiago lives there?" Fami asked.

"Well, not exactly by the falls," his dad answered. "The falls are located within Iguassu National Park. Tiago's village is nearby."

"Oh," Fami said, suddenly lost in his thoughts about the meeting with Tiago.

Peredot noticed her son's sudden silence. "Sweetie, is something wrong?"

Fami shrugged and didn't answer right away.

"Fami?" she pursued one more time.

"I'm just thinking about Tiago claiming he can help me get my sight back. He seems so convinced he can do it."

"He didn't doubt for a second that he could bring back Fami's sight," Seth added.

"He's got all of us believing it's possible," Peredot said.

"We have to try," Rob interjected. "Wouldn't we wonder for the rest of our lives what would have happened if we don't give Tiago a chance? Fami, wouldn't you wonder?"

Fami nodded. "Yes, I would."

"Look," Seth exclaimed, interrupting the conversation. "I think we're here."

Sadie looked out her window at the vast land-scape before her eyes. Deep green fields, dotted with clusters of trees and palms, blanketed low rolling hills beneath a brilliant blue sky. In the distance, she saw two men on horseback and, beyond them, a large, sprawling villa.

"Whoa," she said. "This place is huge."

"You wouldn't believe it, Fami," Seth described the surroundings to his friend. "The house is as big as a church."

"What do you think that is behind the house?" Sadie asked, straining to see what the giant tubes and columns could be.

"I'm sure they'll give us a tour of the place," Peredot told them. "Luciano's wife, Gabriela, is wonderful. You kids will love her."

As they pulled into the circular driveway in front of the home, the front door flew open, and out ran Luciano, his wife, Gabriela, and a girl who looked about Sadie's age.

"Bem-vindos," Luciano called out after Rob parked the car and opened his door.

With open arms, the family greeted them. Gabriela and her daughter greeted Peredot and Sadie with three alternating kisses on their cheeks. Sadie noticed how beautiful the daughter was with her long, raven-black hair and smooth, bronzed skin.

"Sadie," Gabriela addressed her, "this is my daughter, Alessandra. She is twelve years old." She turned to her daughter. "Why don't you take Sadie and show her your room?"

Alessandra nodded her head and turned back toward the house.

The two girls walked inside, stepping on breathtakingly beautiful marble-tiled floors. The foyer was elegant and inviting. Off to one side was a formal living room; on the other side was an office. Ahead of them towered a large, wide stairway. The stairway led to a long hallway with doors on either side.

"I'm sorry, I don't know any Portuguese," Sadie told Alessandra.

"My parents have made me learn English," Alessandra replied. "We travel to the United States often."

"I thought your family was moving to Argentina," Sadie said.

"Yes. We have . . ." Alessandra thought for a moment, "cows there."

"Oh. Is your father also a rancher?"

"Yes," Alessandra exclaimed. "Rancher. Sorry, I still don't know all the words."

"Are you excited to move?" Sadie asked as they paused in front of a doorway.

"It is hard," Alessandra said. "I have friends here. This is home."

"We might be moving too," Sadie told her. "I know exactly how you feel."

Alessandra smiled at her. "I'm glad you came to visit."

"Thanks. Me too."

After just one step inside it, Sadie fell in love with Alessandra's room. The walls were painted soft yellow, and there were two enormous windows with window seats. On the seats were dozens of brightly colored pillows and bright orange cushions. The floor where the white, four-poster bed stood was raised, so there were steps leading up to the bed on either side. Right between the two windows were large French doors leading out to a private balcony that overlooked a pool with water slides.

"Whoa! You seriously have your own water park."

Alessandra looked pleased that Sadie liked the pool. They walked onto the balcony.

"What's that over there?" Sadie asked, pointing to a distant flat area with a tower.

"That is the landing strip for my father's jet."

"Your father has a jet?" Sadie's mouth dropped open.

"Over there," Alessandra pointed another direction, "are stables for the horses. The lake is too far away to see from here."

"Can we go swimming and do the water slides?"

"Sure."

"Wait," Sadie exclaimed. "I didn't bring a swimming suit."

Alessandra laughed. "You can wear one of mine. You look my size."

They walked back inside Alessandra's room, where Sadie noticed a computer desk and study area. On the computer were pictures of Brand X, one of Sadie's favorite rock groups.

"You like Brand X?" she asked.

"Yes, very much." Alessandra rifled through a drawer looking for swimming suits.

"I met a rock star on the airplane coming over. Have you ever heard of Double T? He's a rapper from Great Britain."

"Double T?" Alessandra thought for a moment. "No, I don't know him. I don't really like rap music."

"Yeah, me either. It was just neat to meet him because he might be famous someday."

"We can check and see if he has a website." She pushed a button on the telephone near the computer.

"Yes?" her father's voice said.

"Can I go on the internet? Sadie and I want to Google the name of a rapper she met on the airplane."

"Okay, let me know if you have any trouble finding what you need."

Alessandra pushed the button again, and the intercom turned off. They sat down together at the computer, and Alessandra typed in the name Double T.

The computer clicked and whirred for a moment, then a web page came up with another link to click on to. "That's weird," Sadie said, as Alessandra clicked onto the site.

The computer continued to search for the link.

"Hey," Sadie said, "does your printer do digital photos?"

"Yes. Right here." Alessandra showed her where to put a stick from a digital camera.

Sadie dug into her bag and found her camera pen. "I have a picture of him," she explained. She removed the narrow stick and slid it into the correct slot in the printer. A moment later an image appeared. And even though Sadie couldn't describe it, a strange feeling came over her when she saw it.

Chapter 9
THE REUNION

Alessandra and Sadie both leaned in and studied the photograph, which had been taken on an upward angle and showed Double T's chin, nostrils, and forehead.

"So, that's him?" Alessandra asked.

"Uh, yeah." Sadie shook her head to clear the strange feeling. "It's hard to tell, though, isn't it?"

"Kind of. Should we see if his website came up?" Alessandra clicked on the screen to reveal a photograph of a man singing into a microphone with dancers and a band behind him.

They both stared at the picture for a moment.

"Why is his head so much bigger than his body?" Alessandra asked.

"I don't know. It wasn't like that when I saw him in person. He looks like a bobblehead."

"What is a bobblehead?" Alessandra questioned.

"A bobblehead is a toy that looks like a real person, usually a sports hero or something, but the head is a lot larger than the body and bobs around when you bump it."

Alessandra nodded, then looked back at the computer screen.

"This picture looks familiar. Maybe I have seen him somewhere but I just forgot. Do you want me to print the picture you took of him?"

"Sure, why not?"

The nostril shot of Double T was amusing, and the more the two girls looked at it the funnier it got. They were having a giggling fit when a knock came at their door.

"Alessandra," a woman's voice came, "do you girls want to go swimming for a while? The boys are going."

"Yes, mamãe, we are getting ready," Alessandra called back. Sadie knew a few words in Portuguese, one of which was mamãe—mother.

The two girls forgot about the pictures for a moment, then quickly changed into swimming suits and headed downstairs. Fami and Seth were waiting for them near the door to the backyard.

"It's about time," Seth grumbled. "We've been waiting forever."

"It's my fault," Alessandra said. "I was showing her some stuff on my computer." She opened the door and led the way to the pool and water slides.

In no time, the calm pool became a mass of churning, splashing chaos. One of the other three kids always made sure to wait for Fami at the bottom of the slide, in case he needed help.

"Come on, dude," Seth said to Fami. "Let's race down."

They each sat at the entrance of one of the two tubes and counted down from ten. On "blast-off," they both gave a shove with their arms and flew down the dark, snakelike tunnels. Fami hit the water just seconds before Seth.

"Fami won!" Sadie announced.

"Oh man!" Seth exclaimed.

"But it was close, almost too close to tell," Alessandra said to him.

"Yeah, but there's no doubt," Sadie assured her brother. "Fami won."

"Have you tried going down the slide face-first?" Alessandra asked Seth.

"Face-first . . . whoa, that sounds awesome."

"Come on, I'll show you," Alessandra said.

Seth and Alessandra climbed out of the pool and began the climb up the ladder to the top of the giant slide.

"Is it my imagination," Fami said to Sadie, "or do those two seem to be acting a little odd?"

"Hard to tell with Seth," Sadie said. "He's always odd. But, yeah, if you ask me, I think there's a little something going on. How could you tell?"

"Because he's already gone down face-first. He's just doing it again to impress her."

Sadie giggled. "I can totally see why he would fall for her, but what in the world does she see in him?"

Just then Seth hollered, "Look out below!" as he plopped onto the slide and shot to the bottom, landing with a giant splash in the pool.

Right behind him came Alessandra, who slipped into the water as graceful as a mermaid. Seth was completely impressed.

"Did you see that?" he asked Fami and Sadie.

"Sure did," Sadie answered.

"It was awesome," Fami teased, since he hadn't actually seen it. But Seth was too smitten to notice.

* * *

"So, how was swimming?" Peredot asked as the four children joined the adults on the veranda. They'd all showered and gotten changed for dinner.

"I'd give anything to have a pool like that," Seth said.

"Glad you had fun," Luciano said, wearing an apron and wielding a long pair of tongs. "We thought it might be fun to take you into town to the rodeio."

"They have rodeos here?" Sadie asked with amazement.

"They have cowboys here?" Seth asked.

"Yes, of course. You are in the heart of gaúcho country."

"Are they like the rodeos in America?" Fami asked.

"Your father and I were just talking about that," Luciano answered. "Since he has done rodeos before, he told me much about how they are in America."

"They have similar events, but still, there are a lot of differences. I'm anxious to see this gaúcho rodeio," Rob said.

The two women brought out colorful salads and bowls of vegetables which were placed on the table. A large pot of rice and a pot of beans were also placed on the table, along with a tray of tiny turnovers. Gabriela explained that they were called pastéis and were filled with meat, vegetables, and scrambled eggs. They didn't sound all that great, but Seth still tried one and didn't stop until he'd eaten five. Meat from the barbecue was also served, dripping and sizzling on the platter. From that point on, the conversation turned into oohs and aahs over the delicious meal.

"My goodness, Gabriela," Peredot exclaimed. "I must get your recipes. These salads are wonderful. And the flavoring on the meat is—"

WA! WA! WA! The sudden, ear-splitting wail of an alarm filled the air.

Luciano jumped up from the table and tore off his apron.

"Ha! I've been having trouble with some kids trying to steal my four-wheelers and equipment. I'll be right back!"

Gabriela shook her head. "He loves this kind of thing."

In a few minutes, Luciano tore past the group, riding on a four-wheeler. A trail of dust billowed behind him.

"He didn't have a gun with him, did he?" Rob asked.

"I'm afraid so. He would never try to injure anyone, but you never really know who you're dealing with out there," Gabriela answered.

"Does this sort of thing happen very often?" Peredot asked, her concern apparent. She exchanged worried glances with her husband, an action Seth and Sadie noticed immediately. They obviously all had the same thought—was it just teens, or were the sirens announcing other intruders?

"Very rarely. And we do have hired hands that take care of any security problems. But Luciano just loves going out there to try and catch anyone messing with his property."

The dinner table was silent as everyone strained to hear any sound that might indicate what exactly was going on.

"Can we watch a movie after the rodeio tonight, mamãe?" Alessandra asked.

"Certainly," her mother answered. "If it's all right with Rob and Peredot."

The kids exploded in excitement. They'd seen the huge theater room in the basement.

"I guess so," Peredot said. "If it's not too late."

Just then the sound of an approaching four-wheeler caught their attention.

"I wonder what he found," Rob said, jumping to his feet.

Luciano sped by with a wave of his hand and several minutes later rejoined them, breathless and wide-eyed with the excitement.

"What happened, dear?" Gabriela asked him.

"Someone tripped the wire and set off the alarm. Looks like the noise scared them off, but I've got more men coming on patrol tonight, just to keep an eye out."

"What do you think they wanted?" Rob asked, unable to share his concerns with Luciano.

"Who knows," Luciano answered. "The kids nowadays steal so they can sell things to get money. Compared to most places, we have a very low crime rate in our city. Still, the rate is climbing because so many people are poor and desperate. But there's nothing to worry about. I have a state-of-the-art alarm system that will alert us. It's so sensitive that sometimes flying insects will set it off if they're big enough."

With stomachs full and satisfied, everyone pitched in to help clean up the meal.

"Dad," Fami asked his father, "do you think the alarm had anything to do with Bachmann?"

"I don't know, son, but I'm going to do everything I can to find out. We need to be on the lookout for anything suspicious, just to be safe."

With the dishes cleared away, Luciano clapped his hands and rubbed them together briskly with excitement. "I think we're ready for the rodeio!"

Everyone cheered and headed for the door.

* * *

"This is the steer-roping event," Luciano explained to his guests. "It's different from American steer roping because it takes place on foot. You'll notice that the gaúcho will try to rope the two front legs of the steer as it runs around the perimeter of the arena. If the gaúcho does it right, he'll catch both front legs in the lasso and tighten the rope so the steer's legs are cinched together. Then, the gaúcho must plant his heels in the dirt and yank the animal off of its feet. If the gaúcho doesn't do it right, the gaúcho can get jerked right out of his boots!"

"I'd love to see that!" Seth cried.

The crowd in the stands cheered as the herd of steer charged into the arena. The event began, and, one by one, the gaúchos took their turns attempting to rope the animal and get it on its back in the quickest amount of time. The event was exciting, fast-paced, and very entertaining. Even Sadie found herself screaming for each of the gaúchos in their billowy pants and colorful outfits.

"Steer roping is good, but steer cutting is my favorite event," Alessandra told Sadie as the steer cutting started.

In this event, the horse and rider worked as one in an attempt to isolate one steer and pin it against the barrier of the arena. Many times the gaúcho succeeded, but some of the steer were just too crafty and managed to get away, leaving the audience laughing and cheering for the animal instead of the gaúcho.

"What do you think, Rob?" Seth asked Fami's dad. "Which is more difficult? American or Brazilian?"

"I can't decide, but I don't think I could stop one of those steer on foot. Those men are strong," he answered. "How are you girls enjoying the rodeio?"

"It's fun," Sadie answered, noticing people leaving the stands. "But why are we people leaving. Is it over?"

"Not yet," Luciano replied. "We're heading to the main street where the races are held."

Sadie and Alessandra walked in front of the two boys as the group made its way alongside the road until they found a spot where they had a good view of the race.

"Look, here they come," Alessandra exclaimed.

Two horses and riders took off from the starting line and galloped wildly down the street, leaving a cloud of dust behind them. Neck and neck, the horses ran, with one finally pulling ahead and winning by a nose. The crowd erupted in cheers and excitement as another set of horses took their place at the starting lineup.

"That chestnut-colored horse is gonna win," Seth predicted.

"I bet the tan one does," Sadie challenged, glancing back at her brother. Just then, a blinking light on her watch caught Sadie's eye.

"Hey, my watch is flashing."

Seth looked over. "What does it mean? Did you accidentally push a button or something?"

"I don't think so. I haven't finished the manual yet, but I think it either means someone's trying to contact us or the battery is low."

"Who would be trying to contact us?"

"I don't know, but I'm not sure how to answer even if someone is."

"I think you'd better find out as soon as we get back to Alessandra's."

"You know, I'm not the only one who should read the manual, Seth."

"I know."

"Look," she said, showing him the watch. "It stopped."

"We can't do anything until we get back to the house and read the manual. Now, shush, the race is about to start."

* * *

"Okay, Seth, use your wrist more this time, and I think you'll have it," Luciano instructed. Seth had been fascinated with the way the gaúchos threw the lasso, and he wanted to learn how to do it.

Twirling the rope overhead, he focused on the stool, his target, and then let the lasso fly. The rope arched slightly, then landed just off-center of the stool.

"That was it," Luciano exclaimed. "You almost had it that time."

Even Fami tried his best at roping. But instead of having him aim for the small stool, Seth volunteered to be his target.

"Hey," Seth exclaimed when Fami managed to get the rope over his shoulders. "How'd you do that?"

"I don't know. I just got lucky, I guess."

"Maybe I should try and rope *you* instead of that dumb old stool," Seth said, looking out of the corner of his eye to see if Alessandra was watching, which she wasn't.

"Be my guest," Fami said.

Seth tried several times and finally managed to land the rope over Fami's head.

"Yes," he exclaimed. He turned to see if Alessandra had seen how skillfully he'd thrown the rope, but to his disappointment it was too late. She'd gone inside with Sadie.

Chapter 10

Expect the Unexpected

"Why are you wearing that shirt, Sadie?" Seth asked with a high level of agitation. "Nobody knows Double T."

"I don't care. I'm not just wearing it for that. I like this shirt."

Seth shook his head and focused on the scenery passing by. After breakfast the next morning, Alessandra's mother drove them into town to do some shopping while Luciano took Rob and Peredot out to see the farm. Seth and Sadie's parents would be arriving that afternoon.

"Did you find out anything about the flashing light on your watch yet?" Fami asked Sadie quietly. She was looking through the instruction manual for their spy equipment.

"As far as I can tell, the flashing light does indicate an incoming message. But since we didn't know which button to push to intercept the message, we'll just have to wait until another call comes. I told your dad, and he wondered if Beauregard was trying to contact us."

"Why would Beauregard want to talk to us?" Seth asked.

"I don't know. Maybe just to see how we're doing. Or to check up on our training."

"We haven't been doing any of that."

"I know. We probably should figure out a way to do some later," Sadie suggested.

"Gabriela, what are all those little shacks off the side of the road?" Seth asked. He noticed rows and rows of tiny, cement-walled dwellings with tin or clay roofs, surrounded by garbage, overgrown weeds, and dirt roads.

"Those are homes," Alessandra told him.

Seth's mouth dropped open. He took another good look at the tiny, boxlike structures and saw children running around. "People actually live there? Our gardening shed back in Germany was bigger than those."

"Many people live in homes like these," Gabriela explained. "In fact, most of the people in our branch live in this area. They first build the main room with the cinder block, then as they have the money, they add on rooms," Gabriela told him. "If you kids don't mind, I need to drop something off at the Relief Society president's house on our way downtown. You can see inside.

Some of these homes aren't as bad on the inside as they look on the outside."

Seth and Sadie exchanged looks. They'd been around a lot of different cultures, but neither of them had seen conditions quite like the ones out the window of the car. They knew they were blessed, but seeing how people lived here made them realize just how blessed they were.

Gabriela turned off the freeway and onto a road leading into one of the neighborhoods. The road changed from asphalt to cobblestone, making the ride bumpy and dusty. Children ran barefoot in the street as dogs followed at their heels. On fences and tree branches, anywhere possible, people hung plastic grocery bags filled with garbage. Gabriela explained that this was how their trash was collected. She continued driving until the road changed from cobblestone to dirt. She then pulled over in front of a home with a fence around it.

"Why don't you come in with me? I'm sure Sister Silva would love to meet you. She has a son on a mission and a daughter at BYU. She loves to practice her English on Americans."

Everyone piled out of the car and stood outside the gate, where Gabriela clapped her hands loudly several times.

A voice called out from around the side of the house. Moments later, a woman appeared, wiping her hands on a towel. With a big smile and a friendly wave, she welcomed her guests. Opening the gate, she gave Gabriela and each of the girls the traditional three kisses on their cheeks and shook hands with the two boys. Gabriela made the introductions and beckoned them inside the home.

Because the day was so warm, Sister Silva had standing fans blowing throughout the living room. Gabriela explained that hardly anyone had air conditioning and that many relied on the use of fans.

Seth looked at the large TV in the corner and the rest of their meager belongings. The cement floor was cracked and crumbling, and the furniture was old and worn, but the home was clean and welcoming. Sister Silva was friendly and very excited to meet them.

"Can I get you something to eat or drink?" she asked. "I've got a pig's head in the oven that's ready to eat."

"Oh, no," Gabriela said quickly. "We're fine."

"A pig's head?" Seth asked with amazement.

"Oh, yes. Do you like pig's head?" Sister Silva asked.

"I don't know, I've never had it before."

"Then you must try some. It's very delicious." Sister Silva got to her feet and invited them into the kitchen. She got out a plate, a carving knife, drinking cups, and a large bottle of Guaraná soda pop, a favorite in Brazil. She also set out some crackers.

Gabriela offered to pour the Guaraná while Sister Silva went to the oven and opened the door. Slowly she pulled out a tray and carried it to the table. Sure enough, there on the baking sheet was the golden-brown baked head of a pig, complete with ears and snout.

Sadie felt a wave of nausea wash over her, but Seth looked on with fascination as Sister Silva took the knife and began slicing the pig's cheek. Each slice of meat was mostly fat, and she placed it upon a cracker and offered it to them.

Seth was the first to accept. He popped the whole thing into his mouth and chewed it up.

"Please," Sister Silva said, offering the plate of food to each of them. Sadie took one, staring at it. She couldn't do it. She just couldn't do it.

Just then, she noticed the cat peaking out from underneath the kitchen table. While the others were busy eating and drinking, Sadie quickly tipped her cracker and let the fat slide off onto the floor next to the cat. The cat quickly gobbled it up.

Forcing herself to at least eat the cracker, Sadie popped it into her mouth, chewed, and swallowed as quickly as she could. Then she washed the taste down with the soda.

Seth was on his third cracker when he suddenly stopped chewing, his eyes growing wide. He pointed at the wall.

Everyone looked up to see a four-inch-long black scorpion crawling nearly two-thirds up the wall.

Without a second thought, Sister Silva removed her flip-flop and gave the scorpion a giant whack. The creature fell onto the floor and squirmed a little before going still. Sister Silva scooped it up in a dustpan and dumped it into the garbage.

Sadie had seen all she could handle.

"Are you okay?" Alessandra asked her.

"I'm not sure," Sadie answered.

Taking Sadie's cue, Alessandra tugged on her mother's shirtsleeve to indicate they needed to go. Gabriela then spoke in Portuguese to Sister Silva, who nodded, then hurried from the room. A moment later, she returned with a church manual and several papers.

Forgetting about the children, the two women walked to the front door engaged in conversation. A loud clapping from the road caught their attention. Everyone turned to see the missionaries standing by the gate.

"Elders," Sister Silva exclaimed with excitement. She quickly invited the two young men into her yard. The elders stood before them with big smiles on their faces. "This is Elder Tyler and Elder Weston," Sister Silva introduced. The missionaries shook hands with each of the women and then with the kids, asking them their names and introducing themselves. "The missionaries have come for dinner," Sister Silva told her guests. "Which reminds me, Elder Weston, I have finished hemming your pants."

"Thank you," he answered.

"Elder Weston has grown almost two inches since he came on his mission," Sister Silva explained. "These two missionaries baptized my husband two months ago."

"I like your shirt," Elder Tyler said to Sadie.

Sadie smiled and glanced at Seth. "Thanks."

"So, are you going to visit anywhere else while you're in the country?" he asked.

"Yes, we're going to Iguassu Falls," Seth said.

"You are?" Elder Weston exclaimed. "My best friend is serving there. Maybe you'll see him when you're there."

"What's his name?" Seth asked.

"Daniel Chan. He's Chinese, but he's from California. He likes to tell everyone he's Jackie Chan because of his name and because he knows karate," Elder Weston told them.

"We'll watch for him," Seth said.

"Tell him hi from me," Elder Weston requested. "And tell him it's his turn to write."

The kids promised and said good-bye to Sister Silva and the missionaries. Sadie felt bad for them having to eat pig's head for dinner, but they didn't seem to mind.

* * *

While they waited for their parents to arrive later that evening, the four kids went out on the front lawn. Seth had been skeptical when Alessandra suggested they play soccer, but he'd quickly learned that he was out of her league. She played better than any kid he knew back at school in Germany. She was fast, handled the ball well, and was very aggressive.

A car pulled into the driveway, rescuing Seth from complete humiliation just before Alessandra made her fifth goal against his single goal.

"They're here." Sadie jumped up at the sight of the car. She grabbed Fami's hand and led him along.

The doors of the car flew open, and out stepped their parents, their expressions anxious and excited. They soon gathered their children into their arms, grateful to be reunited. They also introduced themselves to Luciano, Gabriela, and Alessandra.

"We're so happy you could join us," Luciano said. "Please, come inside. You must be exhausted."

There was nonstop chatter as the kids told their parents about all of the things they'd been up to. Seth and Sadie both had questions about their home in Frankfurt, but their father didn't want to discuss it in front of the group.

"So, how do we like the soybean farm so far?" Mr. Fletcher asked. The adults began to talk business, and the kids quickly lost interest. Since they hadn't yet found time to work on their spy training, and since there was nothing else to do, Seth figured now was as good a time as any to practice their skills. Especially if Beauregard was trying to reach them and would most likely ask if they were practicing.

"Hey," Seth announced to the other kids, "I have a great idea. Let's go outside and play a game." Sadie and Alessandra looked at each other and smirked. They wanted to go up to her room and listen to music and talk.

Seth noticed Sadie's reaction and knew she didn't understand what he was suggesting. "Remember that game we learned in summer school?" he asked his sister.

"We can't play that here, can we?" she asked. "What about Alessandra? She doesn't know all the rules."

"We can teach her," Seth said. "And remember, we brought all that equipment with us to help us play the game." He looked at Alessandra who seemed a bit confused by their discussion. "It's kind of a high-tech game."

"What do you call it?" she asked.

He smiled and said, "Spyhunt."

Chapter 11
Spyhunt

Sadie wasn't surprised when Seth "volunteered" to take Alessandra as his partner. He acted like he was being noble to take on the rookie, but neither Sadie nor Fami believed it for a second.

"So we're the first chasers?" Fami asked.

"Right," Seth replied. "It would be best if we could get to the farthest point of your land, Alessandra, then we'd have the whole property to use."

"I can get one of the farmhands to take us down to the field by the tennis courts and stables," Alessandra offered.

"Perfect," Seth said. "And you have your equipment ready?" he asked Sadie.

Sadie knew exactly what he was talking about. During the game he would hide an electrical device that looked like an iPod but in reality was used in training to practice locating and diffusing bombs.

"We're ready," she said. "But you should know, we'll catch you before you get a chance to even climb up the ladder to the water slide." This was the spot that they had chosen as their goal.

Seth laughed. "Whatever, Sadie. We'll probably have time to take a nap while we're waiting for you two."

"We'll still give you five minutes, then we'll start after you," Sadie told him. "And no cheating."

Seth's mouth dropped open. "I don't cheat. I'm just resourceful."

"Call it whatever you want," Sadie said.

"Just turn around and cover your ears and close your eyes," Seth said. "We'll see you in a few hours. Gee, Alessandra, I bet we'll have time for a sandwich or something while we're waiting for these two."

"One, two, three . . ." Sadie started counting.

Seth and Alessandra took off running.

Sadie and Fami turned their backs and covered their ears so they wouldn't hear which direction they went. Checking her watch to see if the time was up, Sadie noticed the flashing light again. "I hope I can remember how to do this. I'm supposed to push the *Mode* button." She pushed the button, and a variety of options appeared on the watch face. As she scrolled through them, the word *Messages* appeared on the list. Choosing this option, she was given the choice to either send or receive messages. She chose the *Receive* option and waited to see what happened next.

A high-pitched beep sounded, then a man's voice said, "T-1, contact Top Dog immediately."

"Whoa!" Fami exclaimed. "That's Beauregard. Do you know how to contact him?"

"I think so," Sadie said as she pushed the button to activate the message option again. Her hands shook, and she had to push the button twice to bring up the *Contact* option. As soon as she made her choice, the dial lit up, and a green light circled the dial rapidly.

Another high-pitched beep sounded, startling Sadie so much she nearly dropped the watch.

"What was that?" Fami said.

"I think I'm supposed to leave a message." Taking a quick breath, Sadie spoke into the face of the watch, "Top Dog, this is T-1. We received your message." Then she added, "Over," and pushed the button again, hoping that sent the message.

"Now what?" Fami whispered.

"I don't—"

"Hello?" a voice from the watch sounded. "T-1, is that you?"

"Beauregard," Fami whispered.

"Yes," Sadie answered. "This is T-1."

Beauregard answered brusquely. "I tried to reach you kids yesterday, but you didn't answer your watches."

"We weren't sure what the flashing light meant," Sadie admitted.

"We instructed you to read the manual," Beauregard said. "But that's beside the point. We've tried to contact you and your parents because we've been notified that one of you is carrying a tracer."

"A what?" Sadie asked.

"A tracking device," Beauregard said with measured patience.

"How do you know, sir?" Fami asked.

"Your watches are equipped with sensors that detect when you are being tracked or followed by a tracer. Someone in your group has been planted with a tracking device, which means someone is following your every move."

"Bachmann," Fami and Sadie exclaimed together.

"Exactly. Sadie, could you have your father contact me right away?"

"Yes, sir," Sadie said.

"Good. We're positive all calls are being monitored, so I chose to contact you on your watches instead of your father's satellite phone because your watches have high-level security."

"I'll tell him, sir. Anything else we need to know?"

"Not right now. I'll handle this through your father. He can reach me via your watch or on my security phone. He knows the codes. I'm sure everything's under control, but in the meantime, you kids try and find where that tracking device has been planted."

"Yes, sir," Fami and Sadie said together.

"Top Dog out."

Fami and Sadie sat in stunned silence for a moment, then Fami's wits returned. "We need to find Seth and Alessandra, then go tell our dads."

"Right," Sadie said, shaking her head to jar her brain back into action. She couldn't imagine how a device had been planted on them, but thank goodness Beauregard's men had discovered it. That only meant one thing, though.

Their location wasn't secret anymore.

* * *

Fami and Sadie thrashed through the long grass on their way back to the ranch house. They didn't have time to look for the electronic device Seth and Alessandra planted because, once again, their game of Spyhunt had become a reality.

Breaking through the barrier of trees and hedges that surrounded the backyard, Sadie and Fami continued running until they heard yelling.

"Hey! What are you guys doing?"

It was Seth, and he wasn't happy with them.

"We can't play anymore," Sadie hollered back.

"What? Why not?"

"Just come in the house, Seth." Sadie couldn't keep yelling. She was out of breath from running across the enormous property. The kids slowed as they got to the stairs leading up to the deck.

"Wait for us," Seth hollered from the pool.

Fami and Sadie caught their breath while they waited for Seth and Alessandra. As soon as her conversation with Beauregard had ended, Sadie had racked her brain for any possible way a tracking device could have been planted on them.

Seth and Alessandra raced across the lawn and caught up with them. "What's going on?" Seth insisted.

"We just spoke with Beauregard," Sadie told him.

"What? How?"

"That beeping light on my watch indicated a call from Beauregard."

"So, what did he say?"

"They've discovered that we have a tracking device on us and every move we make is being followed."

"You're kidding!"

"No," Fami said. "We have to tell our dads right now."

"Okay, hold on, you guys," Alessandra said. "What's going on? It sounds like you're playing the game still."

Seth, Fami, and Sadie all stopped. Each of them knew that for Alessandra's protection, she shouldn't know what was going on. But it was too late. She'd already heard too much.

"I'll explain later," Sadie said. "Right now we have to find our parents."

* * *

"We've been through every possible inch of luggage and clothing," Rob said. "I don't see anything."

"Still, we can't take any chances. I think we need to destroy everything here, then we'll be certain," Dave Fletcher suggested.

Rob nodded. "You're right. We can't take chances."

"Luciano's already got his men standing by to start a fire. He says it's not unusual for them to have bonfires to burn weeds and garbage, so no one should get suspicious."

"Have the children gone through all their belongings and taken out what they need to keep?"

Dave nodded. "We've examined each article they're keeping to make sure they aren't bugged. Peredot and Amanda went with Gabriela to purchase more clothes and personal items for the kids. I feel terrible about destroying their belongings, especially after the fire took so much, but it's our only choice."

"Let's get this over with then," Rob said.

* * *

The kids waited for their fathers in the kitchen and had already eaten some sandwiches and were snacking on fruit and cream-filled cookies.

"Mmm, those look good," Dave said as he took one of the cookies.

"Well?" Seth asked.

Dave took a small bite of the cookie. "We weren't able to find a tracking device," he said. "It could be as small as a watch battery or a piece of wire. Even with Cleopatra's help we didn't find it."

"You kids don't remember anyone tampering with your luggage or any of your personal effects at the airport?" Rob asked them.

"Just Tiago, but both of the bags were checked out at the police station," Fami told his dad.

"Then we have no choice. We have to destroy everything just to make sure," Dave told the kids. "I'm sorry, but you kids understand we can't take any risks. We'd better go find Luciano."

"I can't believe this," Sadie said as the two men left the kitchen. "I'm going to go find Alessandra."

Seth watched his sister leave, then looked at Fami, whose expression was one of sadness and concern. "What's up, Fami?"

"With all of this stuff going on, I'm just wondering if we're still going to be able to go see Tiago. I know there's more important stuff going on than me getting my sight back, but I hate to pass up this chance to try."

"Oh man, I didn't even think about that. But I don't know why we won't be able to go see Tiago once we get rid of the tracking device."

Fami nodded slowly. "I hope so."

"As soon as our dads come back, we'll talk to them about it, okay?"

"Okay," Fami said.

"There's something else I want to ask them," Seth stated.

"What's that?"

"I want to know if we're going to buy this farm," he said. "It's awesome."

"No kiddin'. They said we'd only have to come and live here over our summer vacations if they decide to buy it."

"All right! It's a lot more fun here than in Germany."

"Yeah, but if we live here, I'm not eating any more pig's head."

"You didn't like the pig's head?"

"Are you joking, Seth? Sadie told me she fed hers to the cat."

"I didn't think it was that bad."

Fami pulled a face.

Chapter 12

A Picture Is Worth a Thousand Words

Once the plane leveled out, the *Fasten Your Seat Belt* sign went off. Seth looked down the aisle to see when the flight attendants were bringing them something to eat.

"Hey, Dad, do you think it worked?" Seth asked. "Do you think we destroyed the tracking device?"

"If it was in any of your belongings, I'm sure we got it. And remember, it passed the Cleopatra test," he assured his son.

"Yeah, if Cleopatra didn't find it, then it must be gone," Seth said. "Just like I wish that ugly autographed shirt you're wearing was gone," he told his sister.

"I didn't have time to change into one of my new shirts before our plane left. I didn't really have time to tell Alessandra good-bye either." Sadie felt bad that they had to leave so suddenly.

She had grown close to Alessandra in the short time they'd been together, and she was really going to miss her new friend. But then, Alessandra and her family were getting ready to go to Argentina anyway, so they wouldn't have had many more days together. Thank goodness for e-mail. At least that way they could stay in touch.

The decision to make the trip to Iguassu Falls had come suddenly. The Fletchers and the Laninghams had discussed their next plan of action and decided that a sudden departure might throw anyone who was following them off their trail. So, with barely enough time to throw all their new things into new suitcases, they packed and said their good-byes. There was a high likelihood they would come back to the soybean farm, but Alessandra and her family would be gone by then.

"This is quite an adventure for you, isn't it, Fami?" Dave asked. "How are you feeling about this?"

"I'm trying to not get my hopes up, but I am also trying to have faith that it's going to work. I'm kind of confused inside."

"Understandable," Dave replied. "I think you're taking the right approach. Still, if this works, Tiago and his people will get credit for this medical breakthrough and help their village."

"What if it doesn't?" Fami said.

"Well, son," Fami's dad said, "then we've had a fun jungle adventure and lost nothing in the process, right?"

"I guess." Fami reached down under his feet to check on Cleopatra in her cage. He then checked on the black case, which was under the seat in front of Seth. After it was switched by accident in São Paulo, all of the kids worried something might happen to it again.

"When do we get there?" Seth said. "I'm starving."

"Your mother brought some snacks. Why don't you go see what she's got?" his dad suggested.

Seth was glad to get up and stretch his legs. The plane ride had taken them from the Porto Alegre airport back to São Paulo, then west to Iguassu Falls. Seth would be glad when they got there.

Walking up the aisle to where Peredot and his mom sat together, Seth held onto the back of the seats to keep himself steady. He accidentally bumped against a man's shoulder when the plane hit some turbulence. "Sorry," Seth said.

The man gave him a scathing look, his dark eyes glowering beneath bushy eyebrows. His thick mustache and the snarl on his lips sent a chill through Seth.

Moving quickly to the row where his mom sat, Seth glanced back one last time at the man whose face was now covered by the newspaper he was reading.

"What a grouch," Seth said under his breath.

"Hi, sweetie," Seth's mom said when she saw him.

"Hi, Mom. Got anything good to eat?"

"I brought some sandwiches and some treats for you kids." She dug through her carry-on and produced a bag with sandwiches, chips, and candy bars.

"Awesome! Thanks, Mom." He reached out for the bags.

"Make sure you share. There's enough for your dad and Rob too."

The plane bumped again, and the *Fasten Your Seat Belt* sign flashed on.

"You'd better go get in your seat," his mother told him.

Seth nodded and turned around to head back to his seat, then noticed the grouchy man looking at him over the top of the newspaper.

Turning away, Seth found a different route to his chair by going through the flight attendants' quarters and around to the other side of the middle section of seats.

"Look what I found," he announced as he sat down between Fami and Sadie.

Seth pulled two sandwiches out of the bag and handed them to his dad and Rob. He also gave them each a bag of chips.

"You hungry, Sadie?" Seth said, offering her a sandwich but hoping she'd decline.

"That looks great. I'm not really hungry right now . . ."

"Yes!" he said.

" . . . but I'll save it for later, when I am hungry," she finished.

Seth sneered but didn't say anything else. He split the rest of the chips and candy bars with Sadie and Fami, then took a big bite of his sandwich.

"Oh!" he said with his mouth full. He chewed quickly and swallowed. "I forgot to tell you about the creepy man I just saw."

"Not again," Sadie said.

"Yeah. He's over there a few rows behind our moms."

"What are we, creep magnets?" Fami complained.

"Is it just your superspy imagination, Seth, or is this man really creepy?" Sadie asked.

"Take a look for yourself and you can decide."

Sadie sat up tall in her seat so she could see over the backs. She scanned the passengers until she saw a man who fit Seth's description. "I see him. He doesn't look all that creepy. More like old and grouchy."

"You'd think creepy if you looked straight into his face," Seth said. "I got an idea."

"Do you mind chewing and swallowing first?" Sadie asked.

Seth pulled a face at his sister.

"Okay, here's the plan. I'll go over there by Mom and use the earpieces to listen in on what he's saying." Seth peeked over the back of the seat again. "He's having quite an involved conversation with the man next to him."

"Just don't do anything to draw attention to yourself," Sadie said.

"I won't," Seth replied with annoyance, getting the equipment out of the case. He discreetly slid the earpiece into his ear, then stood up and made his way back into the aisle.

"Do you think the man is following us?" Sadie asked Fami.

"I don't know," Fami admitted. "Maybe we're just overreacting because we seem to always have someone on our tail. We destroyed every personal belonging we had. There's no way someone could be following us."

"Dad's still going to call Beauregard when we get to Iguassu to see if he can tell if we're being followed."

"That's good," Fami said. "What's Seth doing now?"

Sadie looked over the seats at her brother, who was doing a good job of acting casual and unsuspicious.

"He's just leaning against the seat and talking to our moms," she reported. Then Sadie noticed the man in question unbuckle his seat belt and stand. "Wait a minute. The man's standing up." She took a good look at the man next to him, who wore a baseball cap backward, gold chains around his neck, and a baggy jacket with some NBA team logo on it. He looked mean and tough, like someone who wouldn't want to be messed with.

Sadie slid down into her seat. "He's going somewhere."

"Keep an eye on him."

Sadie watched the man walk down the aisle to the back of the plane.

"What's he doing now?" Fami asked.

"I can't really see him right now," she said. "But here comes Seth."

Seth returned to his seat carrying a bag of M&M's in his hand.

He opened the bag and took a few of the chocolate candies, then passed it to Fami and Sadie. They both remained calm.

After waiting a few minutes, Fami finally could stand it any longer. "So?" he asked.

"Well, I found out . . ."

"Yes?" Fami and Sadie said together.

"I found out that . . ."

They both leaned toward Seth.

Seth lowered his voice. "I found out that the older man had to go to the bathroom."

"What?" Sadie exclaimed.

"That's it?" Fami asked with disappointment.

"That's it," Seth said. "But still, there was something about those two that didn't seem right. I don't know, but for some reason, they seem familiar."

"I've never seen those guys in my life," Sadie said. "Where would we know them from? I'm sure I'd remember them if I'd seen them before."

"I know it doesn't make sense." Seth blew out a long breath of air. "I'm not a very good spy. I can't ever figure anything out."

"You're a great spy, Seth. You're still just learning all of this stuff," Fami assured his friend.

"Yeah, but I need to remember stuff better. Like what these guys look like and who they remind me of."

"Well, while you're thinking about it, would you mind helping me to the restroom?" Fami asked.

"Sure," Seth said. "Anything to make this airplane ride go faster. I'm tired of flying."

The boys left, and Sadie enjoyed a few minutes alone. She was about to doze off when they returned. "You're back already?" she complained.

"Yeah, and you're not going to believe what we overhead the creepy guy saying while he was in the bathroom."

Chapter 13

Into the Jungle

"You listened through the bathroom door?" Sadie asked incredulously.

"We didn't mean to do it, and besides, who knew the guy would be talking to someone in the bathroom of all places."

"Seth still had the earpieces in his pocket, and I wanted to put them on, just to test them," Fami said. "I heard the man talking inside."

"What did he say?"

"He must have been on a cell phone or satellite phone, because he was having a conversation with someone, and we're sure he was the only one in there," Fami said.

"So what did he say?"

"Stuff like where he was and what time his plane landed."

"That's it?" Sadie didn't think they'd found out anything useful at all.

"He also said that he was prepared to do whatever was asked of him. Even *that*."

"Even what?"

"He didn't say what he meant, just that he was willing to do 'even that.'"

"Okay, but just for a minute, let's assume this man is some kind of salesman, not a terrorist out to kill us. Maybe he's going to Iguassu Falls on business and he was talking to his boss who told him that he needed to land an account for the company or he was getting fired. Maybe that's when he told his boss he was prepared to do whatever was asked of him. Even something drastic. That could be possible, couldn't it?"

Seth pulled a face. "Yeah, I guess."

"Or what if he's military and he's being asked to go on a very important mission to save someone's life or even his country?"

"I get your point," Seth told her.

"Yeah, me too," Fami said.

"The man is weird and creepy and acts kind of suspicious, but I think all three of us are hypersensitive to everything going on around us. I mean, really, what is the chance that there are some of Bachmann's men on board with us?"

"Probably not that great," Seth said.

"Then I say we keep an eye on the man but that we also calm down," Sadie told them.

"I can do that," Seth said, happy to have any excuse to put on his special pair of shaded glasses. "I'll do surveillance."

"And I'll keep listening for anything suspicious," Fami said.

"Good. I think I'd better tell Dad what's going on too. Beauregard would be proud of us," Sadie said.

For the rest of the flight, they kept an eye on the strange man and the man next to him, but, to their disappointment, nothing exciting happened. In fact, both men slept until they landed.

* * *

"Good girl," Fami said as he held up the rat and stroked her head. He'd kept her in her cage until they'd gotten off the plane. Now that they were on the ground, he let her out of her cage for a much-deserved break.

"Can I hold her for a minute?" Sadie asked. Even she was amazed at how fond of Fami's pet she'd become. But Cleopatra was such an easy pet to take care of and so incredibly smart, how could anyone not like her?

Cleopatra crawled up Sadie's shoulder and perched there for a moment before crawling across the back of her shoulders.

"Ow," Sadie exclaimed, grabbing the pet and handing her back to Fami. "She's digging into my neck with her claws."

Sadie rubbed the skin on her neck and looked at her fingers. "I'm bleeding."

"Sorry," Fami said. "I don't know why she did that. She's usually so gentle."

"The only time she scratches like that is when she's searching for something or hunting around for seeds," Seth said. "You don't have any sunflower seeds on you, do you?"

"Hardly," Sadie said.

"Speaking of sunflower seeds, I'm hungry," Seth said.

The three kids were sitting on a bench near the baggage claim, waiting for their parents to return with the luggage. Sadie suddenly sat up and whacked Seth on the arm. "Look who's going into the men's room."

"Ow!" he exclaimed. He looked in the direction of the men's room, and his eyes grew wide. "Look who's following him inside," Seth said.

"Who is it?" Fami asked anxiously.

"Creepy man and his buddy from the plane."

"That's a little too coincidental, don't you think?" Fami said.

"No kidding! Those two are up to something."

"Seth, calm down," Sadie said. "Dad told us there was no way any of Bachmann's men could be on that flight."

"Yeah, well, I don't think we should take any chances."

"All right, fine. We'll tell Dad as soon as he gets back. Keep watching and see what happens," Sadie instructed.

They waited and watched as a number of men left the restroom, but none of them were the two they were watching for.

"Kids, come and take your suitcases," Amanda's voice called. "Does anyone need to use the restroom before we leave?"

"That's a good idea, kids," Rob said. "This may be the last indoor toilet you see for a while."

Sadie's expression changed to one of displeasure. "Tiago doesn't have indoor plumbing?"

"Not that I know of," Rob answered. "But we'll be fine. Just think of it as a great big camping adventure."

"Hey, Dad?" Sadie said. "We need to tell you something."

"What is it, sweetie?" All the parents turned to look at the three kids.

"Remember those guys on the plane who seemed kind of suspicious? They just went into the men's restroom."

Dave and Rob exchanged glances.

"Rob and I will go in and check things out, just to be safe," Dave told the twins. "Why don't all of you wait here."

Amanda put her arm around her daughter and pulled her close. They all watched as Rob and Dave disappeared into the restroom. After several minutes, when they returned, Dave was on his satellite phone.

"What'd you find, Dad?" Seth asked anxiously.

"Nothing. They weren't in there," he answered.

"What do you mean they weren't in there?" Seth exclaimed with a stomp of his foot. "We watched every person who left. They have to still be in there."

"The restroom was empty, son."

"I don't get it." Seth shook his head. "How did they disappear like that?"

"I spoke with Beauregard, and he said there hasn't been any indication that we're being followed. Still, we can't take any chances. You kids need to stay together and always be with one of us. You understand?"

The three kids nodded.

"He wants us to call and check in with him often. We should still get satellite service in the jungle."

"I don't want to lose contact with him," Amanda said.

"We won't," Rob said. "We'll make sure of it."

"So, the rule is stay together and keep an eye out. Got it?" Dave addressed the whole group.

"Got it," everyone replied.

"Then I guess this is it. Fami, are you ready?"

Fami didn't answer. He just swallowed and nodded his head slightly.

"Son, is everything okay?" Rob asked Fami.

"I'm just trying not to care what happens so I don't get disappointed."

"Everything's going to work out, honey," Peredot said, giving her son a hug. "Don't worry."

Fami nodded and put a smile on his face. "I know, you're right. I guess I'm ready then."

* * *

"I can hear the power of the water," Fami said.

On the way to Tiago's village they stopped to visit the world famous Iguassu Falls. They could barely hear each other's voices over the roar of the falls.

"This is just breathtaking," Amanda said. "Look over there," she pointed. "There's a rainbow." Sure enough, in front of the large, horseshoe-shaped section of the falls, a rainbow twinkled in the sunlight, suspended in the air above the crashing spray of the water.

"This almost doesn't seem real," Peredot said. "We have to get a picture."

Nearby, a young man with dreadlocks and a crocheted cap pushed another man in a wheelchair.

"Excuse me," Rob said. "I hate to bother you, but would you mind taking a picture?"

"Course not. I'd be delighted," he said with his thick Jamaican accent. He put the brake on the wheelchair and took the camera from Rob.

They gathered into a half circle and waited for the countdown to take the picture.

"Smile," the man announced.

"Wait," the man in the wheelchair said. He also had dreadlocks and a crocheted cap and wore a Bob Marley T-shirt. "There's a shadow on the little girl. She should move to the center between the two boys."

Sadie did as the man said, and he nodded his approval.

"Yes, much better. Now you can take the picture," he instructed his friend.

Everyone gave a cheesy grin, and the picture was snapped.

"Thank you very much," Rob said to both of the men.

"No problem," the first man said with a half wave. He then released the brake on the wheelchair, and both men followed the path that led to some of the lower falls.

"Well, I hate to rush everyone, but we need to get going," Rob said. "We're not that far from Tiago's village."

Sadie reached for one of Fami's hands, and Seth reached for the other. "Come on, Fami, we'll help you."

Together, the three kids walked along a cat-walk that was suspended over the rushing river. They passed dozens of people who were on their way to see the falls. Finally they reached the small train that carried tourists back to their cars. The two families waited in the shade for the train to arrive.

Seth noticed the two Jamaican men they'd met earlier, coming up one of the trails toward the train. The man in the wheelchair pointed toward the restroom, and the man pushing the wheelchair changed directions.

Seth watched as the men stopped just outside the restroom entrance, and then, to his surprise, the man sitting in the chair stood up and walked into the bathroom.

"Hey, Dad."

"Yes, son?"

"Remember those two Jamaican guys?"

"Yes."

"I just saw the one sitting in the wheelchair get up and walk into the bathroom."

"You did?"

"Yeah. Don't you think it's weird that he's in a wheelchair but he can walk?"

"I guess it depends on why he's in the wheel-chair. Maybe he had an injury or something and he couldn't walk all the way out to see the falls. Could be a dozen reasons. I'm glad you're keeping an eye out, son, but I think we're safe. Beauregard would contact me if he thought we were being followed."

The train whistle sounded in the distance, announcing its arrival. Soon, the tiny, open-air train arrived, and swarms of people descended upon it, clamoring for a seat so they didn't have to wait thirty minutes for the next one. Luckily, the Laninghams and the Fletchers managed to squeeze into a compartment together.

Seth didn't notice if the Jamaican men got on the train or not, but he decided to listen to his dad and trust that Beauregard knew what was going on. But it was hard to trust anyone any-more. Until Bachmann, Skordos, and all of their men were captured, he would never be completely convinced they were safe.

Chapter 14

STRAIGHT OUT OF THE MOVIES

"I swear, Fami, it looks just like a place where Tarzan would live." Seth was explaining to his friend in vivid detail how lush and green the jungle was. "Or Indiana Jones. Any minute I could see him running by with a jungle tribe running after him, blowing poisonous darts."

"You can't even see the sky," Sadie told him. "The trees are so tall and the leaves are so thick, they've created a canopy overhead. And look! A monkey. Two monkeys."

"Where?" Seth cried, his face against the window.

Sadie pointed them out to him.

"Whoa, look at all of them," Seth exclaimed.

"There are ferns and bushes and trees as far as you can see," Sadie told Fami. "It's awesome."

"Wait, I think we're getting close," Seth said. "There's a sign and a little bamboo shack."

They watched as suddenly the jungle cleared away into a wide open area, and an amazing jungle village appeared. Some homes were on the ground, made of bamboo and thatched roofs, and some were mere lean-tos built against the large trees.

"Fami, you wouldn't believe this place." Seth quickly described the surroundings to Fami.

"Oh, and here come the people," he said. "Their skin is dark brown, their hair is black, and they're smiling."

"These people are welcoming us to their village. And look," Rob said. "There's Tiago." The crowd of forty or fifty people parted, and Tiago walked through with arms outstretched.

Rob parked the van, and the group clambered out the doors. Tiago greeted each of them with a handshake and a hug.

"Welcome to my village. My people are delighted to have you. We have prepared a feast in your honor!" Tiago announced.

"A feast," Seth said. "Now that's what I'm talking about."

The visitors stood in front of the crowd, who looked at them with curiosity.

"We are honored you are here," Tiago said. "Our village is small, but our hearts are big."

Rob spoke for their group. "Thank you for inviting us to your village."

Tiago translated for his people in their native tongue. They began to cheer. Some men had small children sitting on their shoulders so they could see what was going on. The people were small, not much taller than Seth, Sadie, and Fami. They were thin and wiry, but seemed strong and healthy.

Then, similar to a lei greeting in Hawaii, several women stepped forward and presented each of them with a necklace of leaves and flowers, which they put around their necks. The older woman who put a necklace around Sadie's neck stopped and rested her hand on Sadie's cheek for a moment as she spoke some words to her. Tiago quickly translated. "She said you are as beautiful as an orchid and your eyes are the color of sapphires."

"Obrigada," Sadie said, remembering the word for *thank you* in Portuguese.

The woman smiled at Sadie's reply and nodded. She then stepped in front of Seth and spoke after putting a necklace on his shoulders. Tiago translated. "She says you seem brave and strong. You are a leader."

Seth pulled his shoulders back and stood up straighter. Tiago spoke to the woman, who chuckled and patted Seth's cheek.

She then stood in front of Fami. She studied him for several moments, especially his eyes, gazing into them as if in a trance. Then she placed Fami's necklace gently around his shoulders and said several soft words, almost like a chant. She continued chanting as she touched him on one shoulder and then on the other. Her chanting ceased, and she shut her eyes, tilting her head toward the sky.

Tiago explained the woman's actions. "She recognized Fami as the one without sight. She has just pronounced a blessing upon him requesting the powers of heaven to allow his body to be healed."

The woman spoke again with a low, reverent tone to her voice. She continued speaking for several minutes, growing more animated and passionate as she spoke, before falling silent again.

"She says there is greatness inside this young man. He lost his sight to help him learn to depend upon a greater power, that of the spirit. He has been taught important lessons through his blindness. His sight will return when the Great Spirit is finished teaching him. We will give him the medicine he needs to allow his body to repair his vision, but his sight will only return when it is time."

"So," Tiago announced, "it is time to take you to my house to prepare for the feast." The woman scurried away, and Tiago directed them to get their luggage and follow him.

By now, the steamy heat of the jungle had caused all of them to become drenched in sweat. Every movement was effort because the heat had depleted them of energy. But Tiago seemed perfectly comfortable in the saunalike temperature.

"I need water," Seth said. "Fami, are you dying of thirst or what?"

"Yeah, I'm really thirsty."

Tiago heard them talking. "I have water for you up in my house."

"*Up* in his house?" Fami said quietly to Seth.

Seth shrugged and shook his head. The homes he saw were so crudely built, they looked like they'd tumble down like dominoes if a big wind ever kicked up.

Then, there was Tiago's house.

"This is awesome," Seth exclaimed when Tiago stopped in front of a thick cluster of vine-covered trees and looked up.

"Welcome to my home," Tiago said. "The ladder is around to the side."

"We're going up there?" Peredot said, noticing a structure overhead, fifteen feet off the ground.

"Most of our homes are here, in the trees. During the rainy season, this whole area gets flooded because the river rises so high. But at this time of year, we can live on the ground, so many build temporary homes until the rains begin again. I prefer to stay in the trees. There are fewer bugs but . . . more monkeys."

"The monkeys bother you?" Seth said with excitement.

"Oh, yes. They are smart little devils, but they are friendly," he answered.

Peredot whispered to her husband, who nodded his reply. Rob cleared his throat. "Tiago, do you think it is wise for Fami to be up in the trees like this? You know, without sight."

"He will be fine. My grandmother lived with me for fifteen years before she died. She also couldn't see."

"Couldn't she take the medicine you're giving to Fami?" Peredot asked.

"Her eyes couldn't be fixed because she had no eyes," he answered. "Terrible accident. But she managed well and lived in the trees for many years."

"I'll be fine, Mom," Fami said.

"Good," Tiago said. "Then up we go."

It took some effort with luggage in hand, but one by one, they followed him up the ladder to a landing where catwalks and rope bridges stretched out to other structures in other trees. It was a village built in the branches.

"Over here," Tiago said, leading them to his home. He opened a door into a room that stretched fifteen feet by fifteen feet. In one corner was a television and a computer; in the other was a small refrigerator. Other than a few wooden crates to sit on and a shelf for storage, there wasn't much else inside.

"You have power?" Dave remarked.

"Yes. Only a few of us have power. Even though our people have lived very simple lives for many generations, we still need to be connected to the outside world. The dam being built upstream will soon bring power to our entire village. Now," he swept his arm toward an empty corner of the room, "you may put your belongings over there, and I will get you something to drink."

Out of the fridge, he pulled a liter of bottled water and poured drinks into cups for them.

"Tiago, thank you so much for your hospitality," Rob said. "We appreciate you letting us stay with you, but I have to ask an important question."

"Yes?"

"Are we wasting our time?"

Tiago's brows narrowed. "I'm sorry, I don't understand."

"Bringing our son here."

"Milagre is very wise woman with many special gifts. Her name means *miracle*. She did not say *if* your son's sight will return, but *when*. Perhaps his sight would someday return on its own, but perhaps this is the only way your son could ever see again. I believe you were led here by the Great Spirit. We would dishonor the spirit if we did not fulfill our obligation. We become the hands through which the spirit serves others and performs miracles." He spoke with such conviction that it seemed pointless to doubt. "Would you like some time to rest before we attend the feast?"

"That would be wonderful," Dave said. "We're still jet-lagged from our flight to Brazil. And this heat really zaps the energy out of you."

"Zaps?" Tiago asked.

"Drains," Dave corrected himself.

"Oh, yes. You are not used to our climate. Ninety degrees and ninety-five percent humidity. Very zapping."

He went to a shelf where bamboo mats were rolled and stacked in neat piles. Handing each of them a mat, he told them to make themselves comfortable.

"Tiago," Sadie said. "Do you have internet?"

"Yes, I do. You cannot see it, but I have a satellite on my roof."

"Could I check my e-mail?"

"Of course. Everything I have is yours."

Sadie wanted to see if Alessandra had written her an e-mail. With Tiago's help, she was able to get online and access her e-mail account.

Everyone else stretched out on their mats, hoping to cool off for a few minutes.

"Fami," Tiago said, "this creature you have in a cage, it is not dangerous?"

"No. That's Cleopatra. She's not dangerous at all."

"You will want to keep her close to you. She is probably not used to the ways of the jungle and could become a meal for one of the animals here."

Fami nodded. "Yes, of course I will. Thank you."

"So, Tiago," Dave Fletcher asked, "has there been any more trouble from these men who are opposed to the dam and want to mine gold on your land?"

"They come often and promise jobs and wealth and worldly possessions if we give them what they want. They don't understand that our lives are already how we want them. We do not want to move. We do not want automobiles and brick houses. We are happy just the way we are. I'm afraid they won't leave us alone until they get what they want."

"Your people and your culture have to be preserved," Rob stated. "Somehow we have to get the government involved."

"He's right," Dave agreed. "I have friends in the Brazilian consulate. Perhaps I could speak to them."

Tiago's face lit up. "Yes, that would be wonderful." He bowed his head to them. "Once again, I see our paths crossed for several reasons. Great reasons. Perhaps you will help save our village and the lives of the people who live here."

"I will do what I can for you, I promise." The three men then discussed several options for approaching the government for help and for protection.

Sadie logged on to her e-mail account and was surprised to see not only one message from Alessandra, but three.

Hi, Sadie.

I was so bored after you guys left. I wish you could have stayed longer. We're getting ready for our trip, but I'm not excited. I think I'll check out that site on Double T and see if I can find any more out for you.

Write to me soon and let me know how you like Iguassu, and tell me what you're doing. I'll e-mail you from Argentina when we get there.

Tchau, Alessandra

They hadn't been together long, but Sadie felt a strong closeness to Alessandra and missed her terribly. She clicked on the next e-mail and noticed it had another file attached to it.

Check this out! I knew I'd seen this picture somewhere. E-mail me back as soon as you get this and tell me what you think.

Alessandra

Sadie clicked onto the attachment and two pictures came up, side by side. One was of Double T on stage in front of a microphone, singing with his head tilted back and mouth wide open. The next picture was identical except for one thing. Sadie was so shocked when she saw it that she couldn't even get the words out.

Chapter 15

WHAT'S WRONG WITH THIS PICTURE?

"Sadie?" Seth's voice broke her trance as she stared in shock at the monitor. "What's wrong?"

Sadie couldn't speak. She just pointed at the screen and moved her mouth like a fish in water.

"What?" Seth said, coming over to the computer and looking at the monitor with her. "That's weird. Those two pictures are the exact same, but the heads are different. One is that stupid Double T, and the other one is Big Chill. I know that one's him cause I saw him on TV wearing that same outfit. It looks like Double T is trying to pose just like Big Chill. He's even wearing the same clothes as . . . wait a minute." Seth studied the monitor closely. "That's not even Double T's body. His head's been put on Big Chill's body. I told you he was a fake."

"He is not!" Sadie said defensively, even though she had the same thoughts. She just didn't want to admit it yet. Not until she knew for sure.

"Kids, what's going on over there?" Dave Fletcher asked.

"Dad, come take a look at this," Seth said. He began to explain the whole Double T story. "Sadie thinks this guy is super famous, but look at that picture—the guy isn't even real. He's a fake. And so is that stupid autograph on your shirt."

"No, it's not!"

Their bickering was short-lived. "That's enough," their father said sternly. Then, when they had fallen silent, he said, "Let me see if I have this straight. The man from the airplane who helped you that day at the store in the airport—he told you he was a rap star?"

Sadie nodded.

"Then, you mysteriously got separated from Peredot in the airport and suddenly Double T and his assistant showed up?"

She nodded again with a sinking feeling in her stomach.

"This man signed your T-shirt?"

"Yes."

"Where is this shirt?"

She went to her bag and got out the shirt.

"Rob, come and take a look. Sadie, tell me exactly what happened when he signed your shirt?"

She thought back on that moment in the airport when Double T had come to her rescue. "He offered to sign my shirt, and I let him use my camera pen. He accidentally took a picture of himself with it. I have the picture if you want it." She reached in her bag, pulled out the picture she'd printed off at Alessandra's house, and handed it to her father. Then she continued, "He signed my shirt, checked it out to make sure he liked it, then handed it back to me."

"Rob," Dave said, handing Fami's father the picture, "scan this and send it to my office along with Alessandra's e-mail with the picture of Double T and Big Chill. Have them run a check on this photograph. If this man's up to something, they'll find out."

Rob went straight to the computer to take care of the assignment.

"When you say he checked out his signature, what exactly did he do?" Mr. Fletcher asked his daughter.

"Nothing really. He just held it up and looked at it, then he checked the tag for some reason, then he gave it to me. No big deal."

The look on her father's face made her mouth go dry.

"What?" she asked.

"Rob? What do you make of this?"

Rob scooted away from the computer and held the shirt for a moment. He lifted up the tag and looked underneath, then showed Dave. The two men's gazes locked, and they nodded.

"See that small metallic silver dot?" Dave said, showing the kids, then the wives, then Tiago. "That's a tracking device."

The whole group gasped.

"They know every move we're making," Rob said.

"Told ya," Seth said.

"Dad, I'm so sorry," Sadie said. "I didn't know."

"The question is, are these Bachmann's men?"

"Either way, we've got to get rid of this shirt," Rob said. "They may already know where we are, but we can still throw them off the trail."

"I can't believe this," Sadie said. "I should have picked up on this. At the academy they trained us to notice details." Sadie wanted to kick herself for falling into the man's trap.

"He's a professional," her father answered. "No one else picked up on it either, honey."

"I must alert our whole village to this matter," Tiago said. "We will do everything we can to protect you."

"I should have known," Sadie berated herself. "That stupid scar on his chin I thought was so cute, his stupid English accent. It was all fake, a costume. Just to get to us."

Her brother opened his mouth to say something, but Sadie blurted out, "Don't even say it."

"Say what?"

"Say, 'I told you so.'"

"Maybe later, but right now I'm thinking that you said something important just then."

"I did? What?"

"You said costumes. And now that I think back, I remember those two jokers at the airport, the old man with the mustache and the other man sitting by him."

"And what about those men who took our picture at the falls?" Fami suggested. "The Jamaicans. Did you say something about them?"

"Yeah, the man got up out of his wheelchair and walked. I mean, how obvious is that? These guys aren't just regular creeps, they're undercover creeps."

"I think you kids are right," Dave said. "We're not taking any chances."

"Cleopatra!" Sadie exclaimed.

"What about Cleopatra?" Fami asked anxiously.

"No wonder she was digging at the back of my neck. She knew that bug was there."

"Good girl, Cleopatra," Seth said to the rat, asleep in her cage.

Fami smiled, and Seth and Sadie exchanged proud looks. Maybe this would give them some leads so they could finally help put a stop to Bachmann and his men.

"I'd better get on the phone with Beauregard," Dave said. "We need some help out here. We've put the whole village in danger."

"I will come with you," Tiago said. "My people are good fighters. We have dealt with problems much worse than this."

The three men left, and the others remained behind, sitting in unbelief.

"We just can't get away from these people, can we?" Seth remarked.

"Apparently not," his mother answered. "But you children paid close attention to clues and listened to those inner voices. We are going to be fine now."

She patted her son on the back and gave all three kids a smile. "I guess that spy training is already paying off."

Seth's stomach grumbled. "Aren't we supposed to be having a feast? I'm starving. I could eat anything, even jungle food."

"I've got some granola bars in my bag," Amanda told her son. "That should tide you over until we eat."

"I think someone's coming," Fami said.

A few moments later, Tiago came through the door. "The feast is ready. Please, come with me."

A crowd of voices and laughter filled the air as the visitors followed Tiago along a catwalk through the trees. He stopped and pointed at a rope bridge with one thick rope to walk on and ropes on either side to hold on to. It was only a ten-foot span, from one catwalk to another, but the fact that it was twenty feet off the ground made it a challenge, a challenge the kids—even Fami—were definitely excited about. They'd actually received training on how to negotiate a rope bridge. The trick was to keep the rope steady so it didn't swing and knock them off balance. One by one, the kids made it across, then the two moms. Tiago was impressed by their fearlessness and their abilities, especially Fami's.

The other catwalk led them to another tree with boards nailed into it for footholds. Unlike Tiago, who scampered down the tree like a spider monkey, the rest of them slowly made their way to the jungle floor. "I was waiting for him to make us swing on a vine next," Peredot joked as her feet touched the ground. They were met there by Dave and Rob.

Along a fern-lined trail, the visitors followed Tiago through the steaming jungle heat until the leaves parted and an open area spread out before them, filled with villagers and bamboo tables laden with food. A smoky, sweet fragrance filled the air.

The members of the village looked different than when the visitors had first arrived. Now they looked like they were straight off the pages of

National Geographic. The men were bare-chested, with fabric wrapped around them like a sarong. Around their heads were bands of feathers that poked out like rooster crowns, and their faces were painted with black, red, and white paint. The women were also covered in sarongs that wrapped around their bodies and tied around their necks. They had feathers and flowers tucked into their hair, and their faces were also painted. All the natives wore jewelry made of bones, teeth, and shells around their necks, wrists, and ankles. They were an incredible sight to behold.

Several women handed them coconuts with coconut milk inside to drink as they joined the group. Sadie noticed platters of cut fruit on the table—bananas, coconuts, mangoes, papaya, and many other fruits she didn't recognize.

Bamboo mats on the ground provided them a place to sit around a fire pit, where a roasted pig sizzled over glowing red embers. Behind the pit stood a great samauma tree, the strongest in the rain forest. There, at the base of the tree, was a pile of bananas, coconuts, pineapples, and small gourds filled with honey. Tiago explained to them that this was an offering to the spirit to show respect and to ask for protection for the people of their village, especially from the men who were trying to take away their freedom and the life they now knew.

After making sure the guests were comfortable, Tiago took his place in front and held up both of his hands. The crowd grew silent and allowed him to speak. He made a grand gesture toward the visitors and said a few words that caused the villagers to cheer.

A moment later, a very white-haired, elderly man came forward. He held his hands outstretched, with his palms facing upward. Tilting his head to the sky, he shut his eyes and began to speak, his voice low and melodic. The visitors shut their eyes, recognizing that this man was saying a prayer. Many in the group added some moans and cried out words along with the prayer.

"You may now begin the feast," Tiago instructed them when the prayer was over. "Please," he gestured toward the tables. "After you."

Plates made from strips of palm leaves woven together were handed to each of the visitors, and they made their way along the tables of food.

Seth, clearly the hungriest, began to fill his plate with fruit, some type of bread torn into chunks, and coconut cups filled with soup. At the end of the table was a large platter with a woven bowl upside down over it. One of the women smiled at him and lifted the bowl. There, on the platter, was a pile of cooked tarantulas.

Seth's face went white, and he nearly dropped his plate.

The woman paid no attention to him and lifted one of the spiders from the pile and placed it on his plate. The spider wasn't quite dead, and several of its legs twitched before it finally remained still.

Sadie had to look away, her stomach turning inside out at the sight of the spider. She worried that if she refused it she would insult them, so she focused her gaze on the woman's face and not what the woman put on her plate. Then Sadie followed her brother to the fire pit, where slices of roast pig were being served.

"Remember," she spoke so only her brother could hear, "you did say you were so hungry you could eat anything."

Seth groaned.

Taking a seat on the ground, Seth and Sadie put their plates next to their coconut cup of soup and the other one of milk and waited for the others to join them. No utensils or napkins were offered, so the kids used their hands to pick up the safest thing on their plate, a banana.

Fami finally joined them. "Okay, what in the heck did that lady put on my plate?"

"Try tarantula nuggets. Cooked spider legs. Whatever you want to call it," Seth replied, shuddering at the sight of the spider still on his plate.

"You're kidding. Are we supposed to eat it?" Fami asked with alarm.

Rob leaned over and spoke in low tones. "To them it's a delicacy. They will be offended if we don't eat the food we took."

"I didn't take this," Seth argued. "She put it on my plate without my permission."

"Still, we don't want to offend them," Rob told him. Then he leaned in closer to the children. "But don't think I'm eating even one of those hairy legs either. I figure there's enough bushes and leaves around here to hide stuff under. Just be discreet when you get rid of it."

Amanda, Dave, and Peredot joined them, but none of them had a tarantula on their plate.

"Hey, how did you escape the tarantula?" Seth asked.

"We just said no thank you and she understood. Why did you guys take one if you didn't want to eat it?"

"We didn't know we could turn it down," Seth said.

"They'd rather have you not take it than take it and not eat it," Dave explained.

"I'll remember that next time I'm offered bugs for dinner," Seth said sarcastically.

With his plate filled to the brim, Tiago joined them. Seth worried that with him sitting there with them, they would end up having to eat the spider.

"So, how do you like our food?" Tiago asked.

"These bananas are delicious," Seth said. "Very sweet."

"This soup isn't too bad either," Rob said. "What kind is it?"

"Very good for you. It is made of piranha fish and hearts of palms."

Rob swallowed hard and gave a weak smile. "Piranha?"

"Yes, and this bread," Tiago lifted his chunk of bread, "is something we learned to make from the missionaries."

"The missionaries?" Rob asked.

"The CTR missionaries," he answered. "The missionaries come to us in twos, always in twos, and they teach us about the Great Spirit. We have always believed in a great being who is the father of us all, so we listen to what they tell us. They also have a special book about our ancestors."

"Do you mean LDS missionaries?" Rob asked him.

Tiago laughed. "Oh yes. I am sorry. CTR is easy to remember because they wear rings with the letters *CTR* on them. We invited them to our feast, but it is sometimes difficult for them to get here because they do not have a car."

"That would be cool to meet the missionaries who get to work here."

"Not so cool," Tiago said. "Even at night it is hot. Even when it rains it is hot."

The three kids laughed.

Dave attempted to explain to Tiago about the American use of the word *cool,* but he didn't seem to understand.

"You do not think tarantulas are cool?" Tiago asked Seth.

Seth looked down at his plate and the giant hairy creature he'd attempted to camouflage with his bread. "I don't want to offend anyone, but I don't think I can eat it," he said.

"You receive great strength from eating tarantula. Perhaps you should try it before you decide you do not like it."

Seth felt the contents of his stomach shift upward. He looked at his parents, whose faces reflected the same repulsion he felt. Yet they said nothing.

"See." Tiago pulled off one of the legs and bit off the end. "Do not eat the end with the claw in it." He chewed, then swallowed. "Very good. Now, you try."

At their spy training, the kids had been taught to mentally remove themselves from a situation by a form of self-hypnosis where they concentrated on being somewhere else, doing something other than what they were really doing.

The beach in Hawaii. Seth would take his thoughts to the beach.

Somehow he managed to pull the leg off the large spider and lift it to his mouth. Then, with his eyes shut, he took a bite and immediately focused on the sounds, the smells, and the feelings of being at the beach—walking on the warm sand, feeling the rush of the waves at his feet, smelling the scent of salty seaspray on the air. He could almost feel the rays of the sun on his skin . . .

"Seth!" His father's voice broke through his thoughts.

Seth's eyes popped open.

"You did it, son. You swallowed."

"I did it?" Seth said, wiping the slimy residue inside his mouth with his tongue. "Do I have to have more?"

Tiago smiled. "Congratulations. You are now an honorary member of my people."

"What?"

"Most white men do not have the strength inside to do what you have just done. This shows you are brave and have a powerful mind."

Seth looked at his parents and sister with pride. "Did you hear that?"

Sadie rolled her eyes. Not only did she hear it, she knew she would never hear the end of it.

"I'll try," Fami said.

"Yes!" Seth said, pumping his arm in the air. "You can do it, Fami."

With a little help, Fami also pulled off a leg and took a bite. Seth wasn't sure he even chewed, but it didn't matter. Fami swallowed, then opened his mouth to prove it was empty.

The group of visitors crowded in to watch and cheer.

"Okay, Dad," Seth said. "It's your turn."

"But I didn't—"

"You can have one of the legs from mine," Seth said, shoving his plate toward his father.

Giving his son an unappreciative glance, Dave took one of the legs and held it up to eye level.

"I can't keep watching this," Amanda said, turning her head.

Taking one quick bite, Dave chewed quickly and swallowed, then followed it with a large gulp of coconut milk.

The crowd cheered.

"Dad?" Fami said. "Are you going to do it?"

"I was hoping you wouldn't ask," Rob answered. "I guess this is a good example of caving into peer pressure, something we've always tried to teach you children *not* to do."

"C'mon, Dad," Fami coaxed. "All the guys have to do it."

Sadie suddenly took that as a challenge.

"All right," Rob agreed. "I know I'm going to have nightmares about this." He pulled off one of the legs and shuddered, then took a deep breath. In one quick motion, he bit off the end and gulped it down. The crowd cheered and chuckled at the same time as he pulled a face and shuddered again.

Tiago lifted his arm and the cheering increased. The crowd then parted, and a very small man with a long, gray braid down his back approached. "This is Xanti, the elder of our tribe. He has come to officially welcome you as honorary members of our people."

The man stepped forward, and Sadie felt herself cry out, "Wait!" All eyes were on her, especially her mother's.

"You don't have to do this," her father said.

"Yes," Sadie said, looking at Fami and her brother. "I do."

Tiago nodded, obviously impressed at her desire.

Clearing her throat, Sadie looked at the hairy creature on her plate and had a quick second thought. Then she took her mind back to Alessandra's house when they were having fun on the water slides, gliding down the tubes and splashing into the refreshing pool of water. She concentrated, not losing focus until, with a gulp, she swallowed the mass in her mouth. The crowd erupted, and Sadie felt Seth slap her on the back in congratulation. Her parents looked at her with surprise and cheered right along.

Then Xanti approached. The five who had taken the challenge stood, ready for whatever came next.

Xanti lifted half a coconut shell and dipped his thumb inside, then lifted his hand toward Seth's face and put a streak of black across the boy's forehead and down the bridge of his nose. Next came Fami, then Dave, Rob, and finally Sadie. The black stuff had a disgusting smell, but there was a feeling of pride to be wearing the symbols of being brave and having a powerful mind. Sadie just hoped she had a powerful stomach too.

They were then each given a bamboo blow-dart gun and a small quiver of darts. It represented their initiation and a promise that they would have greater protection from this point on in their lives because ancestors before them would now guard them in spirit.

Tiago showed them two different vines hanging from the trees. One was called a water vine. The natives would cut the vine and drink the water inside when they were in need of a drink. But they only cut the vine when it was necessary. They were very respectful of their rain forest and nature. The children remarked how much like Fami's grandfather and the American Indians these Brazilian Indians were.

Tiago then showed them the milk vine. He warned them of this vine because the juice inside of it was very poisonous. It was used for the tips of the darts, and even just a few drops were deadly.

Once the instruction was finished and the ceremony was over, the crowd trilled a high-pitched sound that echoed through the canopy of the rain forest and between the trees.

It was time for Fami's first treatment.

Chapter 16

WEIRD HAPPENINGS

"It is time," Tiago announced. "Fami, you will join me in front."

Fami turned toward his parents, who both gave him a hug, then let Tiago guide him forward.

All eyes were on the young boy as Xanti cracked open a long green pod and scraped the white insides out with his thumbnail onto a small palm leaf. He then sprinkled some powder on top of that and rolled it around inside the leaf to mix it together. Once it was sufficiently mixed, he presented the concoction, which was about the size of a large gumball, to Tiago.

He picked up the white, gooey-looking ball and said to Fami, "This will stimulate the nerves in your eyes that were traumatized by the lightning and help your brain send signals to your body to regenerate and heal the nerves. You may take it and swallow it whole or you may chew it. Then, you must hang upside down for one minute, rest for a minute, then hang upside down one more minute to quickly increase blood flow to the brain."

Fami's eyebrows narrowed as he pondered the instructions. Then, without hesitation, he took the gooey ball and popped it into his mouth. After several quick chews, he swallowed.

"Now," Tiago said, leading the boy to a nearby tree with low-hanging branches. "You will hang from this branch. As soon as you are done, you must go straight to bed. Your body must focus all of its energy on repairing your vision."

With the help of his father, Fami climbed up on the branch and then rolled down into a hanging position. Keeping track of time on his watch, Rob stayed near in case his son needed him.

"How ya doin', sport?" his dad asked.

"Pretty good," Fami said. "Except my head feels like it's gonna explode."

"We have never had that happen," Tiago said, "but sometimes your nose can bleed. You will also feel a great tingling in your head and behind your eyes."

"It is tingling," Fami said with excitement.

Peredot covered her mouth with her hands, and her eyes filled with tears.

"That is good," Tiago said as he helped Rob get Fami to a sitting position.

Just then a round object dropped out the sky, nearly clobbering Fami in the head, but bonking Tiago on the shoulder. Tiago cried out in pain and shook his fist to the trees. "The monkeys seem to find great joy in throwing coconuts at people. Luckily they cannot lift the larger coconuts. Still," he rubbed his shoulder, "even the small ones do not feel good."

Seth and Sadie looked up to see several spider monkeys scampering through the trees, chattering back and forth excitedly.

"Watch out for them. They are friendly, but their aim is deadly," Tiago said.

Fami hung upside down again and waited, hoping the time would go quickly. He was getting a headache from all the blood rushing to his head, and he was a little worried about getting clobbered by a coconut.

"That should do it," Tiago said as he helped Fami climb down from the tree branch. "We will do this two, maybe three, more times. But now, it is important for you to go rest now so your body can focus on nothing but healing your eyes."

Since they were all exhausted from the trip and the oppressive heat, they were happy to retire for the night. And even though she didn't admit it,

Sadie was a little sick to her stomach and looking forward to hopefully sleeping it off.

"I'll join you in a moment. I'm going to try and reach Beauregard again," Dave said.

The rest of them climbed up to Tiago's house and rolled out their mats.

"That breeze feels good," Peredot said, fanning herself with a leaf she'd picked outside the window.

"I just hope a big wind doesn't kick up," Amanda replied. "I mean, really, how stable are these homes anyway?"

"Actually, they are quite stable," Peredot told her. "These Amazonian tribes have been living in the trees for hundreds of years. The use of bamboo, which is strong and flexible, makes them quite suited to the treetops."

"I don't think I'm suited to the treetops," Amanda responded.

They did their best to get ready for bed and used rolled-up clothing for pillows. Dave finally returned from making his call, and from the worried expression on his face, they knew the news wasn't good.

"Honey, what's the matter?" Amanda asked her husband.

"Beauregard confirmed that we have been followed as far as Iguassu Falls. It will only be a matter of time before those two men find us here in the jungle. We have to get rid of this tracking device, but rather than burn it, he offered a different idea."

"What else could there be?" Rob asked. "If we don't burn it, they'll track us."

"That's right. But even if we do burn it, they'll go to the last place they received a signal. Beauregard suggested we send it to him, then perhaps they will track it all the way back to London. To Beauregard's office. If Rob and I go back into town and stay tonight, we can mail it first thing in the morning. This will also lead those men away from the village."

Peredot's face registered immediate concern.

"It will be fine, honey," Rob told his wife as he took her by the shoulders and looked into her eyes. "Tiago won't let anything happen to you. We'll return as soon as we get that shirt out of our hands. Why don't we kneel down for a family prayer before we go?"

* * *

Seth bent over and looked at his friend hanging upside down. "How ya doin', dude?"

"Do you remember my code name?" Fami said.

Seth nodded.

"I'm starting to feel like a bat."

Seth laughed. "You're almost done. Just hang in there a little longer." Then Seth laughed again at his own unintentional joke.

"Son, how are you?" Peredot asked.

"I'm okay. Is it time?"

She checked her watch, then slapped at a mosquito on her neck. "These things are eating me alive. You've got fifteen seconds."

When his time was done, Tiago helped him down from the limb of the tree. The natives who had attended the healing ceremony lifted their voices in a loud, trilling sound, a plea to their gods.

"Now you must rest," Tiago told Fami.

"But I'm not tired."

"You will be. You just need a short rest, then you will be fine."

Peredot and Seth helped Fami up to Tiago's tree house. They found Sadie there, e-mailing Alessandra. Amanda paced the floor, worrying about her husband and Rob. Certainly they'd had time to mail the shirt by now and would be coming back to the jungle.

"Here," Peredot said, showing them a gourd filled with slimy green stuff. "It's supposed to pro-tect you against mosquitoes. Tiago gave it to me."

"What is it?" Amanda asked, sniffing at the foul-smelling substance.

"Sap from some tree. I figure it can't hurt. These mosquitoes are horrible."

Peredot rubbed some of the sap on her own skin, then on her son's. Just as Tiago predicted, Fami was half asleep when she was applying the sap. He kept pushing her hand away and saying, "That stinks. Let me sleep."

Seth fed Cleopatra, then played hide and seek with her using the training device. But since Tiago had no belongings, there wasn't really anywhere to hide it.

"I'm bored," he said to his mom. "When should Dad get back?"

"I'm sure he'll be here soon," she said unconvincingly. "I can't imagine what's keeping them."

"Can I go down and see what Tiago's doing?" he asked.

Amanda looked at Peredot. "What do you think?"

"I think it would be okay."

Amanda turned to her son. "Just don't bother him or get in his way," she said. "And don't do anything dangerous."

"I won't, Mom," he said.

"Be careful climbing down the tree," she called after him as he left through the door.

When he got to the jungle floor, Seth looked around. Several younger children were taking turns tossing rocks into a wooden pot. They stopped when they saw him. Seth smiled and lifted his hand in a wave to them. They remained still as he walked by in search for Tiago.

A group of women was busy grinding corn, cutting fruit, and shelling nuts. They spoke to him in their language as he approached them.

"Tiago?" he asked.

They looked at each other, then one spoke rapidly and pointed through the trees. Seth pointed the same direction, and they nodded. He lifted his hand in a wave, his personal form of signing "thanks," and headed the direction they'd pointed.

The sound of chopping and men's voices told him he was heading in the right direction, and soon he found the men from the village chopping down bamboo and lashing the long poles together with vines. It looked like they were building a lean-to.

Tiago saw him and smiled in greeting. The other men welcomed him with smiles and unfamiliar words and continued their work. "Would you like to help?" Tiago asked.

"Sure," Seth said.

Tiago showed him which vines from which trees were the strongest to use. Some, Tiago said, were as strong as steel cable and could hold hundreds of pounds of weight. Tiago also showed him how to wind the vines in, out, and around the bamboo poles, then tie them securely. It reminded Seth of Scout camp.

He worked busily, wiping sweat from his eyes with the sleeve of his shirt. As Seth reached for another vine, Tiago's hand shot out and grabbed his arm, jerking it back.

Seth recoiled, looking at Tiago with complete shock. Then he realized what had happened. A long, brown-and-cream-colored snake slowly slithered back into the jungle.

"Lancehead," Tiago said. "Very poisonous."

A shiver shot up Seth's spine. He'd nearly grabbed the snake's tail.

"Always watch for danger in the jungle. One bite, and you would die. No medicine would have time to help you."

Seth nodded but couldn't get the image of the snake out of his mind.

They were about to take a break for lunch when the loud roar of an engine was heard in the distance. "My dad's back," Seth cried.

"No," Tiago exclaimed. "Those engines belong to the commandos. You must hide. Quickly!"

"Why?"

"Because you are an outsider. Hurry!"

Tiago gave an order, and one of the young boys grabbed Seth by the hand and pulled him into the thick jungle growth. They crawled underneath the broad leaves of a low-growing bush, and the boy put a finger to his lips to tell Seth to stay quiet.

Loud, shouting voices could be heard. Seth recognized Tiago's voice, but most of the shouting was from the angry men in the Jeep.

The young boy next to Seth shivered with fear.

The shouting seemed to go on forever, and finally the Jeep engines roared again and sped off down the dirt road through the jungle. Seth and the boy waited for the signal that it was safe to come out, and cautiously they left their hiding place.

The whole village was gathered around Tiago, many of the women clearly upset and crying. Finally, after Tiago calmed them down, the people went back to their homes. Seth remained there with Tiago.

"I must speak to your father. He is perhaps our only hope," Tiago told him. "I must call him."

They climbed to the tree house and entered to find the two women and children white-faced and worried. "Tiago, what was all of that about?" Amanda asked him.

"They are tired of waiting for us to come to a decision. They made threats to my people because we will not move. They do not want the dam and will do whatever it takes to stop it from being completed. All of the other villages have given in to their threats and are moving. We are the only ones who have not conceded. We will not receive protection from them."

"What are they going to do?" Peredot asked.

"I do not know, but I do not think we have much time. Something is going to happen soon. They have warned us. I need to talk to your husbands."

"I thought they would be back by now," Amanda said.

Tiago found his satellite phone and dialed the number but got no answer from Dave's or Rob's phones.

"That doesn't make sense," Amanda said. "They would answer if they could. Are you sure you have reception?"

"Yes, the satellite signal is strong. Perhaps they are on their way and will arrive anytime now. Until then, I will keep calling," Tiago said. "I'm sure you are all very hungry. Please, come down and join us in a meal. The women have prepared food. Fami, how are you feeling?"

"I'm feeling fine," Fami answered. "I'm not tired anymore, and I'm very hungry." He reached for his backpack, and Seth put Cleopatra inside.

Carefully they made their way to the village common area where the villagers gathered to eat. Tiago told them that they usually shared one meal a day with the entire village, and the rest of their meals were done by individual families. The women worked together to share the work around the village; they helped each other wash clothing, gather food, cook meals, and take care of each other's children. It was an amazing sight to see them all function as one unit, making sure that their neighbor had everything they needed as well as themselves.

The meal was surprisingly good. The women had made flat, tortilla-like shells that were filled with a meat mixture. They also had bananas, pineapple, and papaya.

Throughout the meal, Tiago, Amanda, and Peredot took turns calling on the phone, but there was still no answer.

Once dinner was cleaned up, the women set to the task of washing clothes. The visitors were invited to participate. They walked to the edge of a wide river where the women began scrubbing clothes against rocks, using a slimy brown substance for soap. It didn't take long for the village kids to take advantage of being near water, and soon all of them, even Seth, Sadie, and Fami, were splashing around in the water, enjoying the cool refreshment it offered.

Tiago joined them at the water's edge. "Would you like to see the waterfall that's been created by the dam?"

The three kids quickly climbed out of the water.

Tiago called to the boy who'd helped Seth hide earlier that morning. "This is Berto," Tiago said. "He knows the way to the waterfall. I will come in a few minutes and check on you."

"They'll be safe?" Amanda asked Tiago as she beat clothing on a rock.

"It is just around the bend in the river," he told her. "We can still hear them from here."

"Be careful, kids," Amanda told the children, her request quickly echoed by Peredot.

Following a walking trail near the edge of the river, the kids followed Berto as he led them through the jungle.

Chapter 17

DIDN'T SEE THAT COMING

"My shirt is completely drenched with sweat," Sadie said. "Fami, can I get my water bottle out of your backpack?"

They signaled Berto to stop for a moment while Sadie got a drink. The three native children got their drinks right out of the river.

Fami had Cleopatra in his pocket. He was afraid she'd bake inside of his backpack. She was resting quietly, sleeping as they walked along the jungle trail.

The sap they'd rubbed on their skin was a big help against mosquitos, but there was nothing they could do to keep away the other creepy crawlers and snakes that appeared in their path. The native children took it all in stride, not even flinching if they nearly stepped on the thin, slithering body of a snake, but it was all Sadie could do not to scream at the top of her lungs when she saw one. After Seth had told her about the lancehead snake he'd nearly grabbed, she didn't want to have an encounter with one, or any of the other reptiles creeping and crawling around the jungle. Boas, anacondas, pythons, and lance-heads were just a few of the snakes that lived in this area.

Berto led them a little farther until the terrain became rocky and sandy. The sound of crashing water grew louder and louder until they emerged from the thick trees and ferns to the edge of a shimmering pool of water. Far across on the other side, dropping one hundred feet, was a breath-taking waterfall, like liquid silver, cascading down the side of the mountain into the pool below.

"Wow, how beautiful," Sadie said.

Seth described the sight to Fami.

Berto and the others seemed pleased at their reaction. The native kids soon dove into the water with giant splashes. Berto turned and beck-oned them in.

"Is it safe?" Sadie asked, visualizing some jungle creature living beneath the water.

"They don't seem too worried," Seth said. "And it would feel good, just to get our clothes wet."

"Sounds good to me," Fami said. "I'm melting."

"I think I'll pass," Sadie said. "But I'll stay out here and hold Cleopatra and your backpack."

"And my ICIs," Fami said, removing his glasses and handing them to her.

Seth led Fami into the water, and soon they were dipping under and coming up sputtering and laughing. Sadie was tempted enough to wade in knee-deep and get a little relief from the sweltering heat.

As she stood there, her gaze followed the horizon from the waterfall along the lush green hill to the east where the dam was located. Several smaller waterfalls spilled into the thick jungle growth. It was beautiful.

Berto found a thick, sturdy vine hanging from the branches of a tree and began swinging from the shore out over the water and landing with a splash. They could've swum for hours, but Berto seemed to sense when it was time to return. For some reason, Tiago hadn't joined them. Berto said something to the other two Macuxi kids, and they immediately left the water. The one girl, who looked about ten years old, gave Sadie a shy smile and reached up to pet Cleopatra's head. Sadie marveled at how completely different their lives were and wished they could talk and learn more about each other.

Berto and the other boy began walking, then suddenly stopped and began backing up slowly. Stretched across the path was a lancehead, lying completely still.

With a nod of his head, Berto started off in another direction that led them away from the snake. They walked a distance along the path and soon noticed that the trail led them to the dam.

"Why are we going so close to the dam?" Sadie asked.

"I was just wondering that myself," Seth answered. "Berto!" he called.

The boy in front turned, and Seth pointed toward the dam and shook his head.

Berto nodded and put his finger to his lips, wanting them to be quiet.

"I don't like this," Sadie whispered just loud enough for her brother and Fami to hear.

"I don't either," Seth said. "Those men are not going to want a bunch of kids coming around."

Once again, Berto put his fingers to his lips and shook his head, then motioned for them to come along. He then put both hands together and pushed them out away from his body, then separated them and opened his arms wide, pointing one toward the dam and the other toward the direction of the village.

Seth understood what he was trying to say. "I think we need to go ahead to where the trail separates. One way goes to the dam, and the other goes back to the village. We'd better follow him."

"I hope he knows what he's doing," Sadie grumbled.

"Tiago wouldn't have asked him to be with us if he didn't trust him," Fami said.

"I guess you're right. I'll just be glad when we get back to the village. I'll bet Dad is back by now," Sadie replied.

Berto shushed them and began walking again. The little girl followed closely behind, and the other boy helped to hold palm fronds and branches out of their way so they could keep up with Berto.

The sound of men's voices and machinery got louder as they got closer to the dam. Seth hoped they would turn back soon. He didn't have a good feeling about getting discovered by any of the workers or the jungle commandos.

Berto stopped suddenly and crouched down. The others quickly dropped to the ground and listened as a loud engine revved its way past. Seth peeked and saw a large truck rumble along the jungle road. From where they were, they had a clear view of the giant dam. Three turbines within the dam wall looked as though they were near completion.

Another large truck carrying equipment and workers shook the ground as it also rumbled by. The kids kept their heads bent and remained still so they wouldn't be seen. As soon as the truck was out of sight, Berto stood up and motioned for them to follow.

Seth and Sadie hurried along, anxious to get back to the village. Both of them remembered the warning that Tiago had received that morning from the commandos, and they didn't want to be wandering in the jungle if something happened.

"Hey," Seth said, "where's Fami?" He turned back and saw his friend standing in the same place gazing up at the dam. "Berto!" he called. Berto saw that Fami wasn't with them, so he stopped while Seth went back.

"Dude," Seth said, "what are you doing?"

Fami didn't answer.

"Fami, we're leaving."

He got closer to his friend and saw that tears were coming down Fami's cheeks.

"Fami, what's wrong?"

"I saw the dam," Fami said, still staring in the distance.

"What do you mean?" Seth said, noticing that Fami didn't have on his ICIs.

"My vision, Seth. It came back for a minute. I actually saw the jungle, the waterfalls, and the dam."

"Fami, that's awesome!"

"I was waiting to see if it would come back again. But it's gone."

"Yeah, but still, something's happening. Those treatments must be working."

"I know," Fami sniffed and wiped at his cheeks. "Sorry," he said, embarrassed at his tears. "Don't tell anyone I was crying."

"Don't worry."

"But, Seth, I saw something else. Men, up by the turbines."

"Yeah, workers are probably up there."

"They were hanging by ropes, not like they were building or constructing."

"What do you mean?" Seth asked.

"I don't know. I didn't get to see for very long."

Seth studied the dam but didn't see anyone. "Do we have our binoculars in your backpack?"

"Yeah, they're in there."

Seth dug through the pack and found the regular binoculars and quickly scanned the dam. "I don't see anyone by the turbines," he reported, but continued to scan the rest of the dam. "Wait." Something caught his attention. "I do see something. It's a man. I don't think he's a worker. It looks like he rappelled down to the turbine and now someone's pulling him back up. I think something weird is going on."

"What if they're the commandos and they've done something bad to the dam like they threatened to do?" Fami said.

They hurried to the group, and Fami quickly told Sadie what had happened with his vision.

She couldn't help but hug him. "This is such a miracle," she said.

"It is," Seth agreed, "but right now, we have to get back to the village. We have to tell Tiago what we saw."

Berto didn't understand what Seth was trying to tell him, but he picked up on Seth's urgency and took off down the trail at a faster pace until they finally came to the dirt road that led away from the dam.

"What's that?" Fami yelled, trying to run with Seth pulling him by one arm and Sadie by the other.

"What's what?" Seth cried.

"The ground is shaking. Something's coming."

"The commandos!" Sadie exclaimed.

"We have to hide!" Seth yelled. "Berto!"

Seth, Sadie, and Fami dove off one side of the road into the bushes, and Berto and the other two dove off the other side just as a Jeep barreled down the road toward the dam.

"It's going the wrong way," Seth whispered.

"Maybe they're going to pick up the men who were at the dam," Fami offered.

"What do you think those men at the dam were doing?" Sadie asked.

"I hate to think," Seth said. "But whatever it is, it's probably bad. The threats they made to Tiago were pretty serious."

Sadie felt something on her neck and jumped, slapping at her neck.

"What are you doing?" Seth hissed.

Sadie saw that the end of a fern had been brushing against her neck. "Sorry, I thought something was crawling on me."

"Hold still. You're going to give us away," he told her.

They waited until they couldn't hear the roar of the engine any longer.

"Let's go!" Seth whispered. They got back on the road and looked both ways for any sign of unwelcome visitors. "It's safe," Seth said, then he called for Berto.

Berto didn't answer.

"I'd better go look," Seth said, walking across the road to the other side. He thrashed around in the bushes and called for the three kids, but he couldn't find any trace of them.

"They left us."

"No way!" Fami exclaimed.

"I can't see them anywhere."

"At least they'll get back to camp sooner," Sadie said.

"We'd better get going before those guys come back," Seth warned.

The three kids hurried down the road as fast as Fami could keep up. Sadie preferred the road to the jungle trails because she didn't have to worry about snakes and bugs. At least with the commandos there was some warning.

They didn't get very far when they felt the vibration of the Jeep coming back from the dam.

"It's them! Hurry," Seth said, pulling Fami with him off the road. Sadie followed, and just as she turned to dive into the bushes, she saw the slithering tail of a snake. She screamed and jumped back, falling down onto the road.

"Sadie!" Seth yelled, reaching for her. But she couldn't hide fast enough. The Jeep came around the corner just as she scrambled into the bushes.

Chapter 18

BETWEEN A ROCK AND A HARD PLACE

"Oh no," Sadie whimpered. "I think they saw me."

"Then we'd better get out of here," Seth said. "We can hide in the jungle."

Crouching low and moving cautiously, Seth led the way with Fami right behind him and Sadie bringing up the rear.

"Seth, do you know where you're going?" Sadie cried.

"I'm heading for the river. As soon as we find it, we can follow it back to the village. That snake has to be gone by now."

"I hear their voices," Fami said. "They're coming right behind us."

"I don't remember a hill," Sadie panted as they climbed upward. It wasn't steep, but in the heat, she easily noticed they were on an incline.

"I know," Seth said. "I was sure this was the direction of the river."

Forging ahead, they followed the trail, hoping it took them where they needed to go. The trail was overgrown with foliage that made it difficult to move quickly.

"I think I hear the river," Seth said.

"Me too," Fami echoed.

"We're close. We're going to make it," Seth said as he stepped out into the open. Then he stopped abruptly. Fami plowed into him followed by Sadie. Seth grabbed onto the branches of a large bush and fought for his balance. Right in front of them was an enormous drop into the river below.

"Step back," Seth cried.

"What is it?" Fami asked.

"A cliff," Sadie told him. "We found the river. It's just thirty feet below us."

"They're coming," Fami said. "I can hear them."

There was nowhere to go. Seth quickly scanned the area around them. He looked at the stream down below and saw in the distance the waterfall and the area where they'd been with Berto and the others. That was where they needed to be. Across from them, on the other side of the river, was the mountain ledge that created the ridge where the waterfall spilled over.

In that split second of scanning their surroundings, Seth formulated a plan. He quickly unzipped Fami's backpack. Grabbing the instruments he needed, Seth took the zip-line gun and took aim. Targeting a spot on the other side of the river, Seth shot the gun and buried the pointed claw at the base of the mountain. "Here," he said, handing each of them a folded metal barrel with rubber grips.

"You're kidding, right?" Sadie said.

"We can do it," Seth said. "It's not even as steep as what we practiced before."

"Where are those kids?" a voice shouted.

Sadie gasped.

Seth quickly secured the other end of the zip line around a large boulder at the edge of the cliff and fought away the fears that were trying to deflate his courage. But he had to be brave—they all did. And they had to think clearly. It was the only way they'd survive.

The kids huddled together beneath tree branches, hoping the men wouldn't see them and would give up and turn back.

"Here," Fami said, handing Cleopatra to Sadie. "Put her in my pack just in case."

Sadie slid Cleopatra into the pack and began to pray like she'd never prayed before.

"Whoa!" one of the men exclaimed as he shot through the trees and nearly toppled over the edge of the cliff. "Be careful!" he exclaimed to the other man behind him.

The other man stepped cautiously through the dense jungle and crept close to the edge and looked over. "That was close."

"You're telling me? I nearly went over the edge."

"Do you think those kids went over?"

They both looked down at the bottom. "I don't see any sign of them," the taller of the two said.

Sadie noticed that they were both wearing white shirts and ties. They didn't look like jungle commandos.

"Where else could they have gone? This jungle's so thick, there's no way they could leave the trail," the shorter man said.

"I don't know, but I don't see—"

Seth, Sadie, and Fami stopped breathing.

"Actually I do see them. You can come out," one of the men said to the kids.

"We're not going to hurt you. We came to take you back to the village."

"Hey," Seth exclaimed as he stepped out of hiding, "It's the missionaries."

"Uh, yeah," the taller man said. "We thought you guys might need some help."

"Where are your name tags?" Sadie asked.

"Oh," the smaller one said. "We don't wear them here in the jungle."

"What are you doing here?" Fami asked them.

"Well, we were just doing our missionary stuff, and we saw you and thought you might need some help," the tall one said.

There was something familiar to Sadie about these missionaries, especially the tall one.

"Wait," Seth said. "Do one of you have a friend on a mission in Santa Maria? He said to tell you hi."

The two men looked at each other, then the taller one said, "That was probably one of the other missionaries that came here. We can talk more when we get to the village. I think right now we'd better hurry."

"I agree," Seth said. "Come on, you guys."

"Just a minute," Sadie said. "My shoelace is untied." She bent down on one knee to tie her lace and listened as her brother asked the missionaries their names.

"Hurry, Sadie," Seth said.

"I am," she replied, looking up. Both of the missionaries were looking at Seth, who was asking them where they were from. Then she noticed something that made the blood in her veins run ice cold.

On the chin of the tall missionary was a scar—a scar in the exact place and the exact length of that of Double T. These were the men who'd been following them in disguise.

"Gee, Sadie, do you need some help?" Seth asked.

"No," Sadie said, standing up. "I got it."

"Let's get back to the Jeep, then," the short man said. "We've got some water bottles. You kids are probably thirsty."

"You can say that again," Seth said.

The two men turned and began walking back to the road, following the overgrown trail.

"Seth," Sadie said softly enough that only her brother would hear.

He turned and opened his mouth to say something, but she held her finger to his lips.

She made a slicing motion on her chin with her finger.

Seth's forehead wrinkled. "What?" he mouthed back.

"Look at his chin," she said, pointing toward the tall man, who at that very moment turned and saw her.

"What's going on?" he asked.

"Uh, we were just trying to decide which one of you was the senior companion," Sadie said.

"Oh, I am," the tall one said.

"That's what I thought," Sadie said. "See, I told you, Seth."

Seth played along. "Okay, you were right. Big deal." Then he stopped dead in his tracks, his eyes growing round, his face turning pale.

"What?" Sadie said, afraid he was going to give away the fact that they had caught onto these two imposters.

Seth pointed to the ground between the two bad guys and them, as a snake slithered into view. It wasn't the lancehead, like they'd encountered earlier, but he guessed these two guys didn't know that.

"Come on," the short man called back to them.

"Wait," Seth answered. "Do you know what kind of snake that is?"

"Snake? What snake?" The short one looked down and saw the jungle creature and quickly jumped back.

"Hold still!" the tall man snapped.

"I think it's a lancehead, the deadliest snake in the entire rain forest. The villagers told us about them. We need to back away slowly and give it a lot of space or it will feel threatened and strike."

"Okay," the short man said, taking a giant step backward.

The kids also moved back, increasing the distance between them and the men.

"On the count of three," Seth said under his breath, "we turn and run to the zip line. Get your handles ready."

"I hope you guys know what you're doing," Fami said.

"Is this far enough?" the short man asked, obviously the more chicken of the two.

"A little farther," Seth said.

Taking another step backward, they watched as the snake completely stretched across the trail then stopped. Sadie knew without a doubt that this snake was an answer to their prayers.

"One," Seth whispered.

"What's the snake doing?" the tall man called.

"Two," Seth said. Then he called back to the men, "He senses the vibration from our movements. We need to hold still."

The men froze in position and peered at the snake.

"Three," Seth said.

Without wasting a second, the three kids took off running in the opposite direction.

"Hey," the men shouted. "Where're you goin'?"

"Get your handles ready," Seth cried as he ran. He locked his handle into position, then handed it to Fami. "Here, use this one. Give me yours."

Sadie had hers ready, and Seth quickly locked Fami's into position.

"Sadie, you go first and warn Fami when he's about to land."

"Okay," Sadie said, not looking down. She'd worked through her fear of heights during training at spy school, but the thought of falling and landing on the rocks below made her stomach knot with fear.

Hooking the groove in the handle onto the zip line, Sadie braced herself, prayed the line would hold, then took a deep breath and pushed off. The first few feet were terrifying, but once she knew the line would hold and the handle was anchored securely, it would only be a matter of seconds and she'd be at the bottom. Slowing her descent by squeezing the handles, which created more friction on the line, she anticipated the approaching ground and landed with the thud.

A yell behind her told her Fami was on his way.

She waited as he drew nearer, then told him to squeeze on the handles until he slowed enough to make a smooth landing. Right behind him was Seth, but by this time the two men had arrived at the cliff and saw the kids escaping.

"Hang on, Seth," Sadie yelled. "You're almost there."

"Cut the line," Seth yelled. "Hurry."

Whipping out her multifunction knife, she took the steel-toothed wire cutters and, with a great effort, snipped the line.

Seth tumbled into the water, missing the rocks by mere inches.

Sadie screamed and ran for him.

While she fished him out of the water, Fami attempted to use his watch to contact Beauregard and tell him to contact their parents and tell them what was going on. Beauregard didn't respond, but Fami left a message for him anyway. He also activated the global positioning device that allowed Beauregard to track them. Fami then put in the earpieces with an attached VHF antennae that would allow him to hear things from an even farther distance.

"Seth, are you okay?" Sadie asked as she approached.

"I'm fine," Seth said. "My leg hurts, but I'm fine."

"Here," Sadie said, "let's see if you can stand on it."

Seth let out a cry as he put weight on his leg, but he managed to come to an awkward standing position. "I don't think it's broken," he said. "At least I hope not."

"Where did those men go?" Fami asked.

"I don't know," Sadie answered, looking around for any sign of them. "But they're after us."

"Then we'd better get out of here," Fami said. "First, can you check Cleopatra?"

Sadie looked in his backpack and made sure the rat had survived. She also found the binoculars and looped them over her neck.

"I tried to contact Beauregard," Fami said. "Hopefully he'll get the message to our parents."

"We ran off without most of our spy stuff," Seth said.

"We'll be okay," Sadie told him. "We just have to find a way to cross the river."

"It's too rough here," Seth said. "We'll get washed away for sure."

Using the binoculars, Sadie looked for a better place to cross. Up higher, where the river cut through the rock, was a narrow passage where they could easily cross. "We have to climb up," she said.

"Are you sure?" Seth asked. "I don't know if I can."

"You have to, Seth. We can cross up there. It's not that far."

"I'll help you," Fami said. "We can do this together."

"Hey, Sadie, grab me that tree branch right there," Seth said, pointing to a thick branch with a forked end, about four feet long. "I can use that to help me walk."

Sadie grabbed the branch, glad it wasn't very heavy, and handed it to her brother.

Going first, Sadie found plenty of footholds and tree roots to help her climb the sloping terrain. Seth groaned a bit with each step but assured them he was fine.

They finally reached the spot where Sadie had anticipated their being able to cross. But the gap seemed much wider up close, and the drop into the river was much farther.

"Oh no!" Seth cried. "Now what are we going to do?"

Chapter 19

Saved for This Very Moment

"We have to go higher," Sadie said.

"I can't climb any higher," Seth argued.

"Are you sure, Sadie?" Fami asked.

"Yes!"

"Then we have to keep going. You can do this, Seth. I know you can."

"Okay, okay," Seth groaned. "Let's just hurry and get this over with."

They continued to climb, their progress slow but steady.

"We're getting near the top," she said. "Then we'll see exactly where we are and how to cross."

They made it to a large, moss-covered rock where they decided to take a break. They found a water vine, and Sadie cut the vine and took a short drink. Seth and Fami each were able to have a drink before the water ran out.

"How are you doing?" Fami asked Seth.

"My leg is really hurting. You know how I said I didn't think it was broken? Well, I lied."

"We have to keep going, Seth. It's just a little farther."

Seth bit his bottom lip as he propped the stick underneath his arm and said, "Okay. I'm ready."

Sadie had to get a boost from Fami as she climbed over the last boulder at the top.

"Uh-oh, I can hear them," Fami exclaimed, still wearing the earpieces. "They're coming our way." He quickly scrambled on top of the boulder, then, with Sadie's help, pulled Seth up.

Sadie turned around to see where they were and gasped. They were standing at the base of the dam, which spread out before them like an enormous cement wall, the turbines dripping water.

"Oh," Fami cried out, grabbing his forehead in his hands and bending over at the waist. He groaned with pain.

"Fami, what's wrong?" Sadie cried.

"My head. I just got this sudden pain."

"Are you okay?" Seth asked.

"Ow, that hurt. I'm okay now," Fami said, straightening back up. "That was so weird." He slowly opened his eyes, then really opened them, wide with surprise. "Sadie," he said, looking directly at her, then shifting his gaze. "Seth."

Both Seth's and Sadie's mouths dropped open. Then Sadie asked, "You can see us?"

Fami nodded.

"Fami, you can see!" Seth cried.

But the miracle was interrupted by voices from the other side of the river. Before they were discovered, the kids headed for the trees.

"We need to check out what those men did to that middle turbine," Fami said.

"Can you still see?" Sadie asked.

"Yeah, it's still blurry around the edges, but I can see both of you."

"I'm so happy for you," Sadie said.

"Me too, Fami," Seth said.

"Thanks, you guys. But right now there's something important we need to do. Up there, by that middle turbine," Fami pointed, "is where those men were."

Seth squinted and looked at the turbine, but couldn't see anything.

"Here," Sadie said, putting the binoculars to her eyes. "Let me see if I can see anything through these." But nothing showed up through the lenses except a couple of birds perched on the top of the turbine. "Nothing," she said.

"We need to go up there and look," Fami said.

"Please don't say that," Sadie said.

"I don't think I can climb up there," Seth said.

"Then Sadie and I will have to do it," Fami said. "Maybe this is the reason I finally got my sight back. Because Heavenly Father needs my help." Then he corrected himself. "*Our* help to save all these people. Something's going on up there, and it's up to us to do something about it."

"You think it's a bomb, don't you?" Sadie asked.

Fami nodded.

"And what if it goes off while we're up there?"

"Sadie, no one else is here to stop it. We're the only ones."

"Except those freaks who are after us," Seth reminded him. "How do we know they didn't put it there?"

"Because as stupid as they are, they aren't dumb enough to hang around waiting for a bomb that they planted to go off."

Seth nodded. "Yeah, I guess you're right."

Sadie sighed with pure exasperation. "I can't believe this, but I agree. Maybe we are the ones who are supposed to do this. I mean, why else in the world would be we right here, right now? It's too impossible to be anything but divine. Right?"

"Right, and you two had better get moving."

"This is so amazing! I'm sorry, but I still can't believe I can see all of this," Fami exclaimed. "This jungle is so beautiful—the water, the sky, even the dam. It's beautiful. And you two," Fami said. "You look just like I remembered you, only older—"

"Fami," Seth said, "I don't mean to interrupt— I mean, with you being able to see and all—but we've got a bomb on this hand and bad men trying to kill us on this hand. What do you think we should do?"

"Run!" Fami said, looking over Seth's shoulder.

Seth turned in time to see the two men posing as missionaries on the opposite side of the river from them. And they had a gun.

* * *

"I think we lost them," Seth said.

"Good, because we have to start climbing here," Sadie said, amazed at how much quicker they could move with Fami being able to see. "How are you doing, Fami?"

"I'm doing great. Oh," he said, "watch out for that branch."

Sadie ducked just in time to save hitting her head. "Thanks."

They had to climb up the edge of the dam where the concrete butted up against the side of the mountain. If they could get about halfway up, they could walk out across the dam along the walkway and access the turbines.

"It's weird," Sadie said, grabbing another branch and pulling herself higher. "I should be terrified about what's going on, but I'm not."

"Yeah, me either," Fami said. "Seth?" Fami turned and looked behind him. "Hey, what are you doing?"

"I can't keep going. My leg is so swollen, I can't bend it anymore. I'm sorry."

Sadie felt bad for her brother, but they had to keep going with or without him. "We're going to keep going, okay?" she said.

"Okay. I'll try and contact Beauregard. Why don't you leave your backpack and the earpieces with me too," Seth said.

Fami reached up to take the sound magnifiers off his ears but stopped. "I can hear them talking. They're getting close. We've messed up their plans. They thought we were heading back to the village," he reported.

Seth chuckled. "Good. They've messed up ours too."

"Oh, listen to this," he said. "They've been told to get rid of us once and for all."

"Those yo-yos don't know who they're dealing with," Sadie said. "You'd better stay hidden, Seth. Don't let them get you."

"I won't," Seth said. "Hurry, okay?"

Fami and Sadie nodded and started climbing higher.

"It's not much farther," Sadie told Fami as the ledge came into sight. "How are you, Fami?"

"I'm good."

Sadie finally reached the ledge and climbed over the cement barrier. Then, with a small leap, she jumped and landed on the wide ledge of the walkway.

Fami came right behind her.

"Okay," she said. "Let's do this."

* * *

Seth knew there was no way the men could see him. The palm leaves were too thick, and the shadows kept him in the dark. But he could see them—Bachmann's men—dressed pathetically like missionaries.

Knowing he was the only one who could stop the men, he put into action a plan he'd concocted, a plan that hopefully would work, as crazy as it was.

Three little spider monkeys had kept him company while he'd been waiting, and they were extremely curious about the human sitting in their tree. The men were almost directly below him now, and Seth knew what he had to do.

With his three friends next to him, Seth took a small coconut and launched it at the short man's head. It was a direct hit. The coconut bounced off the man's head and smacked the other one on the shoulder.

"Hey!" the tall man said, looking up.

Using all his strength not to laugh, Seth watched as the three spider monkeys began chucking more coconuts at the men. This was obviously one of the monkeys' favorite pastimes, because they found great delight in doing it.

The men saw the monkeys and began to yell at them. Then, the tall man removed a pistol from the back of his pants. He took aim and, just as Seth burrowed deep into the branches, fired off a shot.

"Seth," came Sadie's voice over his watch. He had it turned so low he could barely hear her. "What was that?"

He couldn't answer, but he pushed a button letting her know he would respond as soon as possible.

The monkeys had scattered with the blast of the gun but were coming back for more coconut launching. Seth appreciated these little creatures and hoped none of them got hurt while they were helping him.

Seth then grabbed hold of the vine he'd cut down and placed it on the ground, waiting for the right moment. The tall man moved into place, and the short one stood right behind him. Knowing this was probably his only chance, Seth yanked hard on the vine, and the loop on the ground tightened around the men's feet. Both of them fell, but the short man managed to get his foot out of the loop.

Seth pulled hard on the vine, raising the tall man's legs off the ground. He secured the vine as the man wiggled and squirmed just like a fish on a line.

The short man decided to get some distance between him and the booby-trapped tree that was raining coconuts. But Seth didn't let him get far. Coming out of his hiding place, he took another vine and twirled it around his head several times before letting it fly. To his great astonishment, he managed to throw the rope so it landed right over the man's shoulders. With a yank, he jerked the short man off his feet.

The man yelled and kicked as Seth reeled him in far enough that he could also keep him on the line. Both men hollered and carried on so loud that Fami and Sadie heard them.

"What's going on?" Sadie asked over the transmitter.

"I just had myself a little rodeo," Seth said, rubbing his raw palms on his thighs. "I caught me some scoundrels."

"Your plan worked?" Sadie exclaimed.

"Sure did," Seth answered. "I had a little help from my monkey buddies."

Sadie chuckled, then she went quiet.

"You okay, sis?" he asked.

"I'm nervous," she said. "You know me under pressure."

"Yeah, I do. You can do this, Sadie. I know you can. You ate a tarantula leg. You must be brave."

"Brave, or stupid," she answered, then added, "Thanks, Seth."

* * *

"We're almost there," Sadie told Fami.

"Good," Fami said, his voice betraying his nervousness.

"Fami?" she said, keeping her eye on her goal and not looking down. "What's wrong?"

"It's going," he said.

"What's going?"

"My sight. It's like a fog creeping in, and all I see are the shadows."

"Fami, no," Sadie cried. "It can't. I need your help. I can't do this alone."

"It's okay. I'm here. I can still help. And Cleopatra can help us. If there's a bomb here, she'll find it."

"Okay," Sadie said, pushing away the panic that threatened to cause her a major meltdown. "Let her go ahead of me, then."

They stopped and put Cleopatra on the cement walkway. She sniffed, carefully moving along the ledge at a slow pace.

"Those birds are still there. It's weird they don't fly away," Sadie told him.

"Maybe they've made a nest and don't want to leave."

Sadie looked closer. "I think you're right. I can see something that looks like a nest."

"I hope they don't attack Cleopatra."

"Me too." Sadie watched closely, ready to pounce and scare away the birds if they went after the rat. But they didn't move, and Cleopatra got closer and closer to them until she was within mere inches.

"Fami," Sadie said, "something's weird about those birds."

"What is it?"

"They aren't moving, and Cleopatra is standing on her hind feet and sniffing."

"That's the sign she's found something."

Sadie stepped closer until she had a perfect view of the birds and the nest.

"Good job, Cleopatra. She sure hasn't lost her touch." Then, as Sadie took an even closer look, she figured out what was going on. "Fami, I know what's wrong with the birds."

"What?" Fami asked.

"They're fake. They aren't birds. They're a decoy."

"Why would they need a decoy?"

"Because of the bomb."

"The what?" Fami whispered.

"It's a bomb, Fami." A wave of panic washed over her. She was terrified. "Fami," she started to breathe in short gasps, "this is my worst nightmare come true. I can't do it. I can't hold the lives of all of these people in my hands. It's too much!"

"Stop it, Sadie!" Fami exclaimed. "You have been trained and prepared for this moment. You are the only person who can do it. You can stop this horrible thing from happening."

Sadie shut her eyes and prayed. Her prayer was short and to the point. *Help me, please, Heavenly Father.*

Chapter 20

LOVE THINE ENEMIES

Once she determined that removing the birds and nest wouldn't trigger the bomb, Sadie held her breath and slowly lifted the covering.

The timing device read 15:03.

Why couldn't they have found a bomb with several hours on it?

She swallowed her concerns, determined to focus, to put aside her emotions and her fears and get to work.

"What are you doing?" Seth's voice transmitted over Fami's watch.

"We found the bomb," Fami told him.

"How's Sadie?"

"She's doing great. She's just taking a look at the device to see how it's wired."

"Good. Get that thing diffused so you can come and help me."

"We'll try," Fami told him.

"I'll say a prayer for you," Seth said. "Over and out."

Sadie closely examined the device in front of her and began diffusing it. The bomb was simple but would effectively destroy the dam.

"How are you, Sadie?" Fami asked.

"I'm okay," she said. On the outside, she was sweating bullets, mostly from the heat, but inside, she felt amazingly calm, not like she'd imagine she'd feel in such a situation.

By the process of elimination, she was left with two wires—a black one and a white one. As she followed the path of the black wire, she became more and more positive it was the white one she was supposed to cut.

"Are you okay?" Fami asked.

She nodded, then carefully, once again, went through the wiring mechanism and followed the path of attachment for each wire. And again, it came down to the white wire.

9:14.

Time was ticking away, but this time, the pressure didn't bother her because she knew without a doubt that the white wire was the right one. Her gut told her. Even if she tried to second-guess herself, she couldn't.

"I'm ready," she told Fami

"You're sure?"

"I couldn't be more positive."

"All right, then," he said without any doubt in his voice. "Cut the wire."

Sadie pulled out the snippers on her knife and looked at the bomb. "I can't believe I'm doing this," she said.

Fami noticed the light on his watch flashing. He didn't tell Sadie that Beauregard was trying to reach them because she was so focused on what she was doing and he didn't want to distract her in any way. Besides, even if help was on the way, it would never arrive in time to diffuse the bomb.

"Well . . . here goes." Sadie placed the blades of the scissors on the wire. Then, before the reality of what was going on hit her with full force, with every nerve and muscle in her body tensed and anxious, she closed her eyes and made herself squeeze the clippers.

* * *

Seth looked down at the two men suspended from vines and wondered how much longer Fami and Sadie would be. The bad guys were trying hard to get loose, and he wasn't sure he could hold them off much longer. There weren't any more coconuts in the area, and the spider monkeys had abandoned him.

"Listen, kid," the tall man said. "I promise we won't hurt you. Just let us down."

Seth chuckled.

"Yeah, kid. We'll just leave. We've had enough of this jungle. We'll just pretend we never found you. Just cut us down," the short one begged. "I hate this jungle," he complained to his partner. "I'm sick of this heat, the bugs, the mosquitos, and the coconuts!"

"Will you just pipe down?" the tall man told him.

Seth shook his head. What a pair of bumbling idiots.

"Come on, kid. They aren't paying us enough to put up with this. Just let us go, and we'll leave you alone. Besides, we don't want to meet up with any more of those jungle commandos. They threatened to kill us if they ever saw us again," the short man said.

Seth didn't answer. He couldn't speak. Something he saw suddenly frightened him. Not so much for himself, but for the men hanging from the vines. They didn't know it, but slithering toward them was a large, brown-and-cream-colored lancehead snake. This time it was the real deal.

"Blasted mosquitos," the short man complained, slapping at his arms and neck. "Ow! That's where the coconut hit me."

"Quit your whining," the tall man snapped.

"I can't help it. I've had it with this place!"

Seth knew that even though these men were bad and that they had every intention of killing him and Sadie and Fami, he couldn't just sit by and watch a deadly snake poison them.

"Hey," Seth called down to them. "I don't know how to tell you this, but there's a lance-head snake coming your way. You need to hold still."

"You expect us to believe you?" the tall man said.

"You don't have to believe me," Seth told him, "but I'm telling the truth. And if I don't do something right away, one of you is going to die. Or maybe even both of you."

Both of the men stopped moving.

"I don't even know why I'm doing this. You want to kill me and my sister and my friend." Seth looked away. It just wasn't in him to let this happen. Not if he could do something about it. "You guys don't deserve it, but I'm going to try and save you."

The two men didn't reply.

Seth searched through the palms and ferns until he finally found what he was looking for—a milk vine. Taking the blow dart tube and darts from Fami's backpack, Seth then made a tiny incision in the vine. Small beads of milk oozed out. Seth dipped the pointed ends of the darts in the milk, careful not to get any on himself. Tiago had warned him of the great danger in even the smallest amount.

With a small handful of poisonous darts, Seth went back to see the men and the snake. The snake had stopped moving and was resting just ten feet away.

"I'm going to come down a little closer," Seth said. "Hold still."

"Just hurry," the short man told him.

"I'm trying," Seth replied, trying not to groan out in agony. His leg throbbed painfully with each inch.

Loading the gun as Tiago had shown him, Seth took aim and a deep breath, then blew into one end of the gun. A dart shot out the other end, landing a foot in front of the snake.

The short man looked over his shoulder. "You've got to give it more than that, kid."

"Leave him alone," the tall one told his partner. "Don't make him mad."

Seth took aim again and focused on his target. He needed to deliver a quick blast of air so the dart shot out straight enough and hard enough to penetrate the snake's skin. Pulling in a deep breath, he expelled a short, powerful burst of air.

The dart landed close enough to the snake to make the creature flinch.

"You got to hit it, kid. You're just going to make it mad," the short man said.

Seth ignored his prisoner's comment and took aim again. He only had a few darts left, and he had to be accurate. The man was right—agitating the snake was only going to make it strike. He had to hit it.

Moving down the mountainside another few feet, Seth zeroed in on the snake.

"You're toast," he told it before he sent a blast of air through the tube.

"Bull's-eye!" the short man shouted.

The arrow stuck out of the snake's body while it writhed back and forth, uncoiling itself. Seth couldn't tell if the dart was deep enough to administer the poison or not, which was bad because the snake was heading straight for the two men dangling from vines.

"Shoot it again or cut us down!" the short man shouted.

Seth didn't waste any time. He loaded the gun again and gave another blast of air. The dart flew and pegged the snake right behind its head.

"Good shot!" the tall man shouted. "That'll do it."

But the snake continued in their direction.

Seth knew there was only one thing left to do. Pulling out his pocketknife, he went to the vines and was about ready to cut when the short man yelled, "It's working. Whatever you put on those darts is working. Look!"

Sure enough, the snake had gone completely rigid. Then its body relaxed and went limp. It was dead.

"Just in time," the short man said with relief. "That was some fancy dart blowing, kid."

"Yeah," the tall one said. "Thanks, kid."

* * *

Sadie clamped down hard on the pocketknife and squeezed with all her might. The wire snapped in two.

She gasped, not knowing what to expect. The display on the bomb went completely dead.

Fami froze, listening intently. Then he erupted, "You did it, Sadie. You did it! You diffused a bomb and saved all of these people."

Reminding herself to breathe, Sadie looked again at the display to make sure the bomb was dead. "I did it." She sat down on the ground and pulled in several more deep breaths. "I can't believe I just did that."

"Are you okay?"

"I think so." Once they got back to the village, she would probably collapse, but right now she felt great. "Come on, girl," she said, scooping Cleopatra up in her hand. "Let's get down off of this thing."

Carefully they walked across the walkway to the barrier that separated the dam from the jungle. Helping each other, she and Fami climbed over and landed on the jungle floor.

"I'm so glad that's over," she said. "Mom and Dad are never going to believe this. And Beauregard. He will never believe this."

"You want to tell him?" Fami asked. "He's trying to reach us."

Sadie looked at the flashing light on Fami's watch and smiled. "Yeah, I want to tell him."

Fami pushed the buttons, and a series of beeps sounded. Beauregard's voice came on.

"Fami, is that you?"

"Yes, sir. I'm here with Seth and Sadie."

"We have updated information that the two men who've been following you are somewhere in the jungle. Where are you? Your parents are waiting for you in the village."

"Well, sir," Fami said as he and Sadie kept climbing down to get to Seth, "we've been a little busy."

"Busy doing what? Don't you realize how serious the situation is? With all the trouble those jungle commandos are causing and now with Bachmann's men after you, you are surrounded by danger."

Sadie couldn't help but laugh. If Beauregard only knew.

"Sir," Fami said, "the situation isn't quite as dangerous as it was five minutes ago."

"What are you talking about?" Beauregard demanded.

"Sadie just diffused a bomb that was planted at the dam."

"I couldn't have done it without Fami's and Seth's help, sir," Sadie said over Fami's shoulder.

"Let me get this straight. You found a bomb at the dam, and you've diffused it?"

"Yes, sir," Sadie said. "With nine minutes to spare."

"What about Bachmann's men?"

"Seth's got them covered," Fami told him. "In fact, we're almost to him right now."

"There he is," Sadie said. Then she started to laugh.

"What's so funny?" Beauregard shouted over the phone.

"Hey," Seth hollered, "look what I caught."

Sadie shook her head with disbelief. "You'd have to see it for yourself, sir," Sadie said. "You won't believe it unless you do."

Seth smiled proudly at his work, then started laughing with his sister. Sadie told Fami what Seth had done, and Fami joined in.

"Help is on the way. Hold your position. Someone will be right there," Beauregard said. Then he added, "I don't know what's so funny, but congratulations. And Sadie, good job. I knew you could do it."

Chapter 21

ALL THINGS ARE POSSIBLE

"This will be your final treatment," Tiago said to Fami. "We are honored to help you after all you did to save us, the dam, and our rain forest. And you too, Sadie and Seth." He gave Fami his last ball of medication and then gave a different concoction to Seth.

"You're welcome," Fami said, putting the ball of goo in his mouth and quickly swallowing.

"We're glad we could help," Seth said, eyeing the black furry glob that looked like some kind of fungus.

"Go ahead," Tiago encouraged. "It will help your leg heal much faster."

Seth wondered if eating fungus was much worse than eating a tarantula leg. "Here goes," he said, feeling like he was putting a caterpillar in his mouth. He gagged as it hit the back of his throat, but he quickly swallowed and took a long drink of water.

Fami hung upside down from the tree, and Seth rested on a bamboo mat, letting the jungle medicine do its work.

"How do we ever thank you?" Tiago said to the two families. "We are forever in your debt."

"It's like you said, Tiago," Rob told him. "Our paths crossed for a reason. You are giving Fami his sight. That is something we could never give him. You are helping Seth's leg to heal. These are great blessings in our lives. And it's a blessing that the kids were able to help you, your people, and your rain forest. It's all very remarkable."

"Yes. With the Great Spirit, we know all things are possible."

"We believe that too," Rob said.

"Perhaps we need to listen to your missionaries," Tiago said. "I think they have much they can teach us."

Rob nodded. "And it will bring you and your people great joy."

Tiago gave each of the parents a hug, then Seth and Sadie.

"Hey," Fami cried. "What about me?"

They all laughed as Tiago hugged Fami, who was still upside down.

* * *

"This is our final look at the falls," Dave said.

"I'm kind of sad that Luciano decided not to sell his soybean farm," Seth said. "Brazil is a pretty neat place."

"Well, things didn't work out so well for him in Argentina. For now, they are staying in Brazil. We'll go back to Germany and put things back together there," Dave told his son.

"And those two guys who were after us? What happens to them, Dad?" Sadie asked.

"With their testimonies and the information they're sharing, it's possible that we could finally capture Bachmann. Their willingness to give us all the details they have on Bachmann is critical in bringing that man and his organization down once and for all. Then we will finally be free from him."

"Then I'm glad I didn't let the snake get them."

"They're still amazed that you saved their lives," Dave said.

"Something inside of me just couldn't watch them die."

"They were also amazed that you kids were actually able to disassemble the bomb. And now the Brazilian government finally understands that they need to protect their tribal people from these jungle commandos. A lot of good things have come out of our trip here to Brazil."

"Hey," Fami exclaimed. "Look at the rainbow."

"Can you really see a rainbow through your glasses?" Seth asked.

"I'm not wearing my glasses," Fami answered.

All of them turned to look at Fami. Tears were streaming down his face. Soon, those around him also had tears in their eyes. His vision would most likely continue to fade in and out, but the moments when he was able to see, he didn't take for granted. It was a miracle, and just as Tiago said, with God, all things truly were possible.